Re

Rival

The Will Stover
Sports Series

By CE Butler

For Arielle, the achiever

Chapter 1

Will Stover quickly ducked and, seeing an opening, threw a hard right fist into Bryce Lockin's left cheek. The shot stunned Bryce and he stumbled before lunging to return a punch. It caught Will on the back of the head, blurring his vision for a second before Will regained control of himself.

"Back off, Bryce!" Will shouted, his voice cracking. "This isn't going to solve anything and we're both going to get in trouble for it!"

"You're not getting out of this that easy!" Bryce yelled back, matching Will's volume. He pulled Will to the ground, which was the last place Will wanted to be with the heavier, more muscular Bryce. Two sharp blows into Will's ribs momentarily took away his breath.

"Are we fighting or wrestling?" Will thought to himself. All he wanted was for this to end.

"WILL!"

It was his mother's voice.

"It's time to get up!" she said for what he realized was the second, or maybe the third, time. "You have practice before school today and I doubt that you want to miss your first day."

Will wasn't certain if he more welcomed the end of the make-believe fight or the beginning of his freshman basketball season. The dream, he realized, likely shadowed his dread of being on the same team with Bryce again.

At the insistence of Coach John Peterson, Will had been promoted to the varsity football team that fall. While leading the Baltic High Bearcats to their first state championship in more than 20 years, Will had quickly realized a downside. There was some jealousy, perhaps even some animosity, from his ninth-grade classmates.

It hadn't been his decision. Will had tried to explain that. Only his best friend, Cam Show, had seemed to understand. Most of the others wanted to give Will more space than he was comfortable with; placing him on a sarcastic pedestal he didn't want.

His success as the starting varsity quarterback had been great to share with the upperclassmen. To those in his class, though, the state championship was the end result of their classmate being in the right place at the right time.

"Kyle could have done the same thing you did with *that* team." Bryce had spewed those hurtful words in the middle of an English class the two shared during the first semester. "Coach just didn't give him a chance and when he finally did, he got hurt."

Kyle Britton was the 'other' quarterback on the football team. When Will had played a horrible first half in the team's season opener, Kyle had come on and nearly led the team to a victory. Kyle's broken hand, though, had given the job back to Will. The Bearcats hadn't suffered another loss. It was now obvious to Will that everyone wasn't thrilled with his stardom.

The only other downside to Will's move to the varsity was his missing the junior high football season with the teammates he'd always played with. Younger brother Ty, a seventh-grader, had stepped in and led the team to an undefeated season. That only seemed to add to the drama, however.

Now, Will was again able to walk to practice and board the bus for away games with Cam and his other teammates. Problem was, that included Bryce.

The two had gotten along fine until they entered junior high and friends began competing with each other for positions on sports teams and spots within the student government. What had always been a good, if not great, relationship between the two had quickly soured as Will rose above the others in nearly every area.

"You remember how to do this?"

Cam tossed Will a basketball and resumed tying his shoe. Will felt the leather of the ball and thought of how huge it felt compared to the football he'd been tossing the past six months. Basketball was easily his weakest sport, though he'd always been good enough to manage a spot in his team's starting lineup.

Basketball season couldn't have come soon enough for Cam.

Having barely broken the 6-foot height barrier since the beginning of the school year, Cam had already established himself as the go-to guy on the ninth grade team. The Bearcats were off to a 4-0 start, having begun their season while Will and the varsity football players made the playoff run.

"I think so, but it'll probably take a couple weeks to get used to it again," Will said. It would be interesting to see where Will would fit in with a team that had already played together for more than a month, especially a team that was yet to lose a game.

A group of players made its way to the court from a separate dressing room. Coach Kurt Hammett, who coached both the junior high and the varsity basketball teams at Baltic, didn't believe in cutting players who wanted to be on one of his teams. All couldn't possibly dress out for each game but Coach Hammett found room on the practice court for nearly two dozen players.

The players heard the whistle before Coach Hammett had even closed his office door. He soon appeared from around the corner and had his team's attention.

"You guys know the drill. Get started!"

Coach Hammett looked more like a wrestling coach than a basketball coach. He was, though, the longest-tenured coach at the school and his team had earned a state championship just three years before.

"Will, you have everything you need?" Coach Hammett moved quickly toward Will as he asked the question. Not waiting for an answer, he turned and jogged to the other end of the court, where mostly seventh and eighth graders were stretching.

Will stepped into a layup line and waited his turn. He caught a quick look from Bryce across the court. It wasn't a bad look but it didn't look like Bryce was inviting him over for ice cream, either. He suddenly remembered the dream and felt somewhat ashamed, like he was seeking out trouble with his rival.

After five minutes of the drill, the groups switched ends of the court. The younger players took over the layup drill while Will's teammates stretched under the basket.

There was another glance from Bryce, this one fiercer than the first.

"I'm imagining things," Will mumbled to himself.

With another game the next day, Coach Hammett had a light practice schedule. The starters and key substitutes ran through a series of plays while the others watched. Ty had played a lot in the team's first four games, most of which Will had watched. Cam was definitely the star of the show, though. He'd led the team in scoring in three of the games.

Practice soon ended and the team showered, dressed and headed to class. Twenty-four players tried to crowd through the gymnasium exit at once. Will was given a hard bump from behind.

"This team is just fine without you here."

"Hello, Bryce," Will said as he veered off toward a distant classroom.

Chapter 2

Bryce Locklin had seen himself as a quarterback when he arrived at the junior high school in Baltic. He had played the position on a pee wee football team in another town before his family relocated, with his dad as the coach.

As Will remembered it, that lasted about one-third of the team's first practice before Cam had taken over the position. One thing led to another and Will eventually replaced Cam as the quarterback. Apparently, Bryce had never recovered from the disappointment.

And, he blamed Will.

It was all Will could do to keep his thoughts on his studies as he maneuvered through advanced classes in English, History, Geometry and Spanish. Bryce was one of the starters on the basketball team and Will wasn't ready to deal yet with where he would fit into the mix.

And he wasn't going to spend all his free time worrying about it.

After a glorious fall with the varsity football team, stepping back into the junior high ranks was something of a blow to Will's ego. He admitted that to himself, even if he wasn't the best basketball player around – even in his own class.

The junior high basketball season had three highlights: the Greenfield Invitational Tournament, the county tournament and the district tournament. There was no state championship to win on this level and Will was having trouble finding the same motivation he had in football.

He did know he wanted to be in the starting lineup by the time the Bearcats headed to the Greenfield tournament. Will would have an audience there and he'd pictured the scene several hundred times in his head.

Shelby Sparks, who had won Will's heart during the football season, had moved to Greenfield over the Christmas break. They were still an item, technically speaking, but he worried constantly about how long things would last. Greenfield was just an hour away and Will spent a lot of time there, even before Shelby's family moved. His father owned an automobile dealership in Greenfield and had been a standout football and baseball player at Valley Tech University, which was the hub of the town.

Still, an hour's drive was a long way for a 14-year-old, especially one who didn't yet have a car or a license.

He'd met several of Shelby's new friends and had competed against many of her new classmates. She admitted she'd been given a hard time – all in fun, she said – about dating a boy from a rival school. If his team showed up to the tournament and Will found himself on the bench … talk about a blow to his ego!

And, it would probably embarrass Shelby.

Will just wasn't certain which starter he would replace. He was strictly a shooter and had given up becoming a terribly reliable ball handler or a strong rebounder several years ago. But, he could shoot. Up until now, that'd been enough for coaches to keep him on the floor.

"Focus on my strengths," Will reminded himself as his Spanish instructor attempted to teach the conjugation of verbs. "Well ... focus on my strength."

Baltic cruised to its fifth consecutive victory the next night at Sparta. Fortunately, the outcome was never in doubt after the first quarter. With a big lead already in hand, Coach Hammett sent Will into the game to begin the second quarter. Oddly enough, he replaced Cam as Coach decided to try a smaller lineup.

It took four Baltic possessions before Will touched the ball. He immediately gave it up as a Sparta defender sprinted out to guard him. His pass found Bryce, of all people, open for an easy layup. On the way back to the other end, Bryce made no attempt to acknowledge the nice pass, something players usually did when they were the recipient of a pass that directly led to two points.

After three more possessions, Will began to notice he'd received a pass from every teammate on the floor, except one. The Bearcats ran something that resembled a motion offense and it was important for the ball to move from one player to another quickly, with sharp passes.

When the ball came to Bryce on two occasions, he'd re-started the offense and swung the ball to the other side of the

9

floor, away from Will. When it happened again on the next possession, Will wondered if Coach Hammett was noticing.

He glanced to the bench but all he saw was another wave of Bearcats ready to check in. He'd played four minutes and hadn't put up a single shot. It was going to be difficult to win a starting spot if he did nothing to draw Coach Hammett's attention.

Leading by 25 as the second half began, Will found himself in the game at the same time as Ty. He hadn't realized it until then, but the two had never played on the same basketball team. Ty, easily the best athlete in his seventh grade class, would be playing solid minutes for the team for the rest of the season. His game was a lot like Will's. He was clearly one of the better shooters on the team, which could be a problem as Will fought for playing time.

At least now, Will thought, he might get open for a shot. He was fairly certain his little brother wouldn't try to freeze him out of the offense.

The ball moved around the perimeter with ease. It appeared the Sparta team had given up and was going through the motions at this point. Will found himself open against the Mounties' sagging zone defense and launched a three-pointer, his first shot attempt of the season.

The ball found the bottom of the net and Will repeated the shot the next trip down the floor, this time off a pass from Ty, who had driven through the defense and found his brother rotating to the corner.

A new group of Bearcats was sent into the game. Cam had played most of the first quarter and several minutes in the third. He'd already gotten used to the fact that he'd be sitting and watching a lot this year after he helped his team build big leads.

He and Will spent the final six minutes of the game sitting together, watching as Ty controlled the game. Coach Hammett, trying to keep the score to a reasonable margin, had instructed the Bearcats to run their offense for 40 seconds each possession before attempting a shot.

"I think Ty could have scored 20 just in this quarter," Will said to Cam.

"Your little brother can flat shoot it, that's all I know," Cam said. "He's been playing great."

Almost as an afterthought, Cam realized he hadn't said anything about Will's performance in his first game.

"Coach is going to have to find some minutes for you, too, if you keep shooting the ball the way you did tonight," he said.

"I hope so," Will said.

Bryce ignored Will as the team changed clothes and headed to the bus for the ride home. He had scored 12 points, second only to Cam's 15. If he was bothered by Will's success shooting the ball, he didn't show it.

"Did you notice what was going on when Bryce and I were in the game together?" Will whispered to Cam as the bus pulled away.

"Not really," Cam said. "What are you talking about?"

"Notice I hardly touched the ball?" Will asked.

"A little paranoid, aren't you?" Cam said. "Hey, we won by 30 and we're undefeated. Not a good time for drama, Will."

Will immediately regretted the selfish thoughts. He couldn't help but think he was going to need an ally through this, though.

Chapter 3

"You want to head over to Valley Tech for their game?" Cam asked the next morning as Will and Ty exited their mother's car beside the side entry to the Baltic High main building. "They're 6-0, you know. They're playing Pullman on Saturday. It's supposed to be one of the best games of the year."

"Can't," Will answered. "We have some family thing we're not supposed to miss. I'm not sure what it is. I'd much rather be watching basketball, though. Especially in Greenfield. I haven't seen Shelby in three weeks."

"Well, you'll definitely see her next week," Cam said. "It's the biggest junior high tournament of the year. I'm thinking I've got a shot to make the all-tournament team. Should have made it last year."

Cam still hadn't gotten past last season's misfortune. After averaging 22 points through the first two games , Cam went cold from the floor and failed to score as the Bearcats got thumped in the finals. To add insult to injury, two Baltic teammates made the all-tournament team.

"Yeah, I know. I've heard the story," Will said sarcastically.

"Well, I should have," Cam shot back.

"Let's focus on winning the tournament this time," Will said. "Remember? No drama."

"Gotcha," Cam grinned.

"You're going to miss a great game Saturday, though. You sure you can't get out of whatever this family thing is?" he asked. "Of course, if you can't make it, I'll just have to keep Miss Shelby company for you."

Cam laughed.

Will didn't.

"Not funny, especially when I haven't seen her," Will said. "You think I'm dumb for assuming this is going to work out … with her, I mean?"

"Dumb?"

"Yeah. Do you think this is crazy? These things never work out in the long run, ya know?" Will said.

"I'm probably not the guy you need to be asking for advice," Cam said. "You haven't forgotten the Micah Cronsky incident, have you?"

Will laughed. No, he hadn't forgotten. No one had forgotten, which might be a reason Cam was having trouble moving forward in the girl department. After dating for three weeks – an eternity for an eighth grader –Micah's birthday had totally slipped Cam's mind. Later the same week, he unknowingly hit her in the back of the head with a rotten egg. Several hours passed before Cam was told the girl he saw out of the corner of his eye, and then fired upon, was his girlfriend. His parents grounded him, which felt like adding punishment on top of punishment to Cam.

14

Will chuckled again.

"She speaking to you yet?" he asked his best friend of seven years.

"Nope. And, I can't say I blame her."

"Me either," Will said.

The family event was something Will's parents had told him about several months earlier. Unfortunately, the annual Stover family gathering indeed found its way onto the calendar and that Saturday saw Will, Ty and Chelsea reunited in the back seat of their mother's sport utility vehicle, heading toward a state park. The unseasonably warm weather was quite welcomed.

Most of the Stover relatives lived two hours north of Baltic. Occasionally, one would stop in for a quick hello. For the most part, though, everyone kept their distance until time for the annual reunion. Both boys were anxious to see their grandparents. They'd all been in town for the football state semifinal game but then missed the championship game because of a trip the four of them had planned together.

Most of the day, they knew, would consist of the older folks sitting and re-telling stories of which neighbors and friends had married, died, divorced, struck it rich or lost it all. A few cousins would be in attendance but none who were involved in athletics. It made for a long day for both Will and Ty. Chelsea could have fun visiting with anyone. A social event was a social event for her. She was perfectly willing to pose for photos and discuss her college plans with folks who were almost strangers.

After spending a few minutes catching up with the grandparents and saying the obligatory hellos to aunts, uncles and cousins, Will and Ty spotted a reprieve. A basketball goal had been installed since their last visit.

For most families, a basketball goal 150 miles from home with no basketball would be a problem. As a Stover, though, the boys knew sports equipment could always be found in their parents' cars. A quick glance inside the rear of the vehicle proved them correct. Not one basketball, but two. A football, two baseballs and six unopened cans of tennis balls rounded out the collection.

There were advantages to living in an athletic family.

Two female cousins joined the brothers as they headed to the court. After about three shots each, though, the cousins dismissed themselves, insisting there *had* to be something more fun to do.

"One-on-one?" Will asked his little brother.

"How about just some h-o-r-s-e?" Ty answered.

"B-o-r-i-n-g," Will spelled back, mocking the little guy. "C'mon, let's play. To twelve by ones, make-it, take-it."

"Fine," Ty conceded. "My ball, then."

Undersized compared to his older brother, Ty never had much success playing against Will. He was weaker and had to find room to release shots from the outside or he didn't stand a chance. Will knew this, of course, and bodied up against Ty, forcing him to try to drive around him.

So that's what Ty did.

Will reached for a steal and Ty blew by him and easily laid the ball in. He caught it out of the net, grinned at his brother and headed back to the top of the key.

"1-0, big guy," Ty taunted him.

"Long way to go," Will said.

Not wanting to get beat on the drive again, Will backed off slightly. Ty took immediate advantage, drilling back-to-back 3-pointers – counting two points each in this game – for a 5-0 lead.

"Have you even touched the ball yet?" Ty asked with his best tough-guy grin.

"Just play and stop talking so much," Will said. "You won't hit another of those."

Instead, Ty drained two more, building a commanding 9-0 lead.

"If this was table tennis, this game would be over," Ty said, laughing.

Forcing his brother to try to drive to the basket again, Will blocked Ty's shot, recovered it and stepped back to nail a 3-pointer of his own. He was able to shoot over his younger sibling and quickly hit two more long-range jump shots to cut the lead to 9-6.

"Not much to say all of a sudden, huh?" he chanted at Ty, almost daring him to respond.

The brothers finally lost the touch and the game dragged on until Will used his size to get inside and take the lead.

A final 3-pointer sealed the victory for Will.

The boys grabbed a quick lunch and headed back to the court. It took Ty three more games to finally beat his brother. By that time, both had had enough and grabbed seats under a nearby tree.

"Should we go back over and visit? Ty asked.

Will, staring at his phone, didn't reply. He looked stunned.

"Will?"

"Leave me alone," Will mumbled under his breath. He stood and walked toward the family's car.

Chapter 4

A picture is worth a thousand words.

Will stared at his phone, oblivious to his family surrounding him in the car. Cam had attached a short message with the photo he'd quietly taken at the Valley Tech basketball game and sent to Will's cell phone.

"Not sure what's going on here but I thought you might want to see this."

The picture was of Shelby and Bryce sitting together in the arena at Valley Tech. They looked like a happy couple, perhaps planning a date … or already on a date.

After he'd faked heartfelt goodbyes with his relatives, Will had retreated to the car. He immediately texted Cam, who he felt would still be at the game. His text asked for more details. Cam wasn't certain how to respond.

"Man, I don't know," Cam said. "I didn't see them come in together. I saw her, sitting all the way across the arena from me, but she was with Lydia then. Next thing I knew, Bryce was there and sitting next to her. And Lydia was gone."

Lydia was Shelby's cousin. She and Ty had become quite close during the fall but the relationship had simmered, as usually happened with junior high-aged kids.

"I'll talk to her later. Maybe it's nothing," Will wrote back. He was certain he was either being very paranoid or he was trying to convince himself it was nothing. "Have you ever seen Bryce at a Valley Tech game before?"

"Never," Cam said, "and we rarely miss a home game."

Will didn't care to share his concerns with the other passengers. His short reply to Ty on the basketball court had sent his little brother into hiding, not wanting to bother Will again.

Will's worry got the best of him, though. He and Shelby usually texted each other several times a day. More times than not, the messages lacked substance. Typically, it was nothing more than a "Hey, how's it going" …

He began typing, not knowing exactly how this was going to end: "Family reunion finally over … any plans for tomorrow?"

He waited for a response.

Ten miles passed. Then, another ten.

Nothing.

Will was tempted to send another but didn't want to sound desperate. He kept reminding himself that she'd never been dishonest with him. They'd never even had an argument.

Why Bryce?

Of all people, why Bryce?

"How's basketball going, guys?"

It might have been Steve Stover's first mention of basketball since Will began practice two days earlier. During football season, he insisted on a daily report from each son. He wasn't much of a basketball fan, though, and sometimes had to remind himself to inquire about the team.

Both Steve and Alicia made all the games but, with so many of them, failed to greet them with the same enthusiasm they gave football.

"Pretty good," Ty said. "Greenfield tournament is coming up. Everyone seems pretty excited about that. It's cool to finally get to play in something I've only been able to watch for so long."

"You'll still be watching," Chelsea said with a smile. "Unless you guys get way ahead or way behind, that is." Chelsea enjoyed giving her brothers a hard time.

"Now, Chels," Alicia said. "Ty's been doing great. He's only a seventh grader and he's gotten to play quite a bit so far. And, he's done great. I know you're busy but you should really make time for your brothers' games."

"Like they come to my cheer competitions?" Chelsea asked with a sarcastic tone.

"Well-played, sis," Will said.

Finally, when they arrived home, Will was able to focus on something else. He had homework due Monday and didn't

21

want to spend any of Sunday doing it. If Shelby ever responded, he was planning to try to talk his mom into a quick trip to Greenfield on Sunday.

It took an hour to finish the homework and sleep was starting to call. He glanced over at his phone on the desk.

The flashing light told him there was a message.

It was Cam, though.

"Everything OK there?"

"Don't know yet," Will replied quickly. "I'll let you know something when there's something to know."

Before he'd finished typing the last word, his phone beeped for an incoming call. The screen showed Shelby's school photo, taken the previous fall.

"Hey," Will said. The last thing he was going to do was tip his hand that something was wrong.

"Hey, I'm so sorry," Shelby said. "I went to the game and left my phone at home. I just saw that you texted earlier. How was the family reunion?"

"It was good, I guess," he said. "How was the game?"

"Valley Tech won," she said. "It was pretty exciting. Guess who I talked to for the first time ever?"

"Who?" Will asked. As if he didn't know.

"Your buddy Bryce," she said. "He was actually really nice. He said it was the first college game he'd ever been to there. He mentioned that you guys are playing here next week. He said he just wanted to see the arena before he plays in it."

A likely story, Will thought. Bryce and Will had both played in the same tournament the year before.

"That's pretty lame, don't you think?" Will said in a disapproving tone.

"Pretty *lame*?"

"Yeah, it sounds a little weird, doesn't it?" Will said. "It sounds to me like he figured out something to do that would really get to me."

"What are you talking about, Will?"

"It's no secret the guy doesn't care for me," Will said. "Never mind that I've never, in my life, done anything to him. Now, I guess he thinks it's OK to go after my girlfriend."

"He's hardly coming after me," Shelby said with a sigh. "Will, you know me a little better than that, don't you?"

Will figured he was in too deep to get out now.

"I'm not sure," Will said. "It's just that … I don't get to see you all the time. Makes me worry, ya know?"

"Worry about what?" she asked with a shortened tone, letting Will know she was up for the challenge if he wanted to push this.

"Nothing. Never mind," Will said. "You said nothing happened. I believe you. I just don't trust the guy."

"Do you trust me?" Shelby said.

"Yeah, I guess," Will said almost under his breath.

"Will?"

"Yes. I said yes," he answered.

"OK, then. If I'm not mistaken, you asked me if I have plans for tomorrow."

"Yeah, but something came up since the time I sent that," Will said. "I've got to do some things around here for my dad."

"So, I'll see you later in the week, I guess?" Shelby asked.

"Tournament starts Tuesday. I'll see you then," Will said.

They hung up as Ty knocked on Will's bedroom door.

"You OK, bro?" he asked.

"I'm fine, little guy. What's up?"

"You get Coach Hammett's text?" Ty asked.

"Haven't looked at it yet," Will answered.

"Practice tomorrow afternoon," Ty said. "I guess we need a little more work with the tournament coming up."

"Hey, are you worried about me taking away playing time from you?" Will asked. "I mean, have you thought about that?"

"Been thinking about it since the season started," Ty said. "We play the same position. We do exactly the same thing on the floor. We're shooters. It's never been an issue because we've never been on a team together. I thought it would be more fun when we finally were."

"OK," Will said. "I guess the main thing is to keep winning and let the other stuff work itself out," Will said. "That's why Coach Hammett gets paid and we don't."

Chapter 5

The Sunday practice turned out to be more intense than the players had hoped. Coach Hammett split the squad into two equal teams and watched them scrimmage for an hour. Before that, though, there had been a half hour of conditioning, something most coaches wouldn't have dared try just two days before a tournament.

"I don't want you guys getting soft or thinking you're better than you are," Coach had told the team as they ran the bleachers in the gymnasium. "You haven't played anyone yet. That'll change this week. You're going to see some of the best junior high teams in this region of the state. We're going to find out just how good we are this week."

Will had found himself on what he felt was an undermanned team for the scrimmage. Two of the weaker starters were on his team, Ian Smock and Jeffrey Patterson. Ian was the team's point guard. One of the smallest players, he rarely scored but earned his keep by playing great defense and handling the ball most of the time against pressing defenses. Jeffrey was athletic but was still growing and it showed. He was inconsistent, able to score 20 points one game and be held scoreless the next. Just a fraction taller than Cam, he was nowhere near the player Cam was.

Two other reserves rounded out Will's team.

They were facing Ty, Cam, Bryce, another sub named Chris Peabody and the team's fifth starter, Luke Smith. Luke was the team's starting shooting guard and the most likely candidate for Will to replace in the lineup.

Ty, who was perhaps an inch taller than Ian, would handle the point guard duties for his team. Coach Hammett knew Ty could score and saw in the previous game that his skills handling the ball had vastly improved. Maybe Coach was seeing another opportunity for Ty to play.

As one of the taller players on his team, Will drew the task of guarding Bryce, a much more physical player than himself.

"Focus on your strength," Will reminded himself.

On the first trip down the floor, Ty immediately fed the ball inside to Bryce, as if he sensed a mismatch. Bryce caught the bounce pass, dribbled once and turned to shoot. As he did, his shoulder caught Will under the chin, sending Will flying backwards. There was no whistle and Bryce easily dropped the ball in for two points.

Will gathered himself and trotted back down the court. Jeffrey shot quickly and missed and it was time to play defense again. As if he was trying to incite something, Ty went directly back to Bryce. Taking the pass, Bryce turned quickly. Will gave him a little room and Bryce acted as if he was about to duck his shoulder into Will again. Instead, he quickly passed off to an open Cam for another easy two.

Bryce laughed aloud as Will took the ball out of bounds.

"Focus on my strength," Will reminded himself.

Another too-quick shot was put up by Jeffrey and missed but Luke sped in for an offensive rebound, keeping the possession alive. From the baseline he whipped a pass out to Will, who was camped out two feet beyond the three-point line.

Swish.

Now, it was time to keep Bryce from making him look silly, Will told himself. But, it wasn't that easy. Bryce was playing like a guy on a mission and was personally taking the ball straight at Will every chance he got. And Ty was making sure he had lots of chances.

Ty fed the ball to Bryce on the next two possessions. Will played solid defense the first time, stiffening as Bryce tried to back him down toward the goal before finally giving up the ball. The next time, though, Will caught Bryce trying to lean back on him, positioning himself for another pass from Ty. Once Will felt most of Bryce's weight leaning into him, he quickly stepped to the side. Bryce flopped to the ground and Will picked off Ty's pass and headed the other way.

Ty retreated in an effort to slow the fast break. He darted toward the ball but Will switched hands and sped by his little brother. He stopped before the three-point line, faked a pass to a streaking teammate, and drained another long-range shot.

Bryce was still picking himself off the floor on the other end. Will had turned the tables, making Bryce look lost out there. His rival was now fuming, calling for the ball. Ty gave in, sending another pass in Bryce's direction. Will again pressed against Bryce, trying to keep him from turning to face the basket. With the ball in his right hand, Bryce used all his might and gave Will a hard blow into the midsection with his left elbow. The shot sent Will back to the floor. Quickly, he was up and shoved Bryce in the back.

The two came nose-to-nose before Cam stepped between them.

"You guys knock it off!" Coach Hammett shouted as he started onto the court. "This isn't your personal wrestling match. It's my basketball practice. Both of you, out!

"Give me two more in here, right now!"

Will and Bryce made their way off the court, choosing seats at the opposite ends of the bench.

Coach Hammett returned to the bench as the teams resumed the practice game. He took a long look down the bench at Will, caught his eye, and slowly shook his head.

Chapter 6

"Coach say anything to you?"

Cam had joined Will and Ty on the walk home after the practice. Neither Cam nor Ty had said anything about the practice incident until they were almost to their destination. Now, Cam was itching to know what had happened.

"No, he didn't say anything other than what you guys heard," Will said. "It was pretty clear he wasn't happy, though."

"So, what got into you, anyway?" Cam pushed the issue.

"What do you mean ... what got into *me*?" Will said." Bryce started the whole thing. The elbow in the ribs, the laughing ... his only goal today was to get to me."

"I'd say it worked," Ty said.

"Yeah, well you didn't really help matters, little brother," Will said. "Ever heard of letting the rest of your team touch the ball? Like, maybe Cam? He's the best player on your team and you got the ball to Bryce every single time."

"You play your game and I'll play mine," Ty said. The comment stung Will for a second.

"That's how it's going to be, huh?"

"I was running the offense," Ty said. "Sorry that it had to be you ... but everyone on the court knew you would have a tough time stopping Bryce if he got the ball that close to the goal. The best thing for me to do was keep getting him the ball."

"So, sacrifice your brother for yourself." Will was getting angrier by the second.

"I want to play, Will. Bottom line, I want to play," Ty said. "If he's going to give me a shot at playing point guard, then I'm going to do whatever I can to do it. Today, that meant going after you. You'd have done the same thing."

What really hurt was that Ty was right and Will knew it. Once a game or a practice started, there were no friends on the other team.

"Well, there's a lot going on between Bryce and me right now and today didn't help," Will said. "Stuff you know nothing about."

"Will, everyone on the team knows Bryce was sitting with Shelby at the Valley Tech game yesterday," Ty said. "Seriously, everyone on the team knew what was going on out there. Except Coach, I guess, and he'll probably figure it out pretty quickly."

The boys had arrived at the Stover's house.

"Cam, let's go," Will said, pulling his friend away from Ty. "Not really trusting the little guy a whole lot right now."

Monday's practice was the usual walk-through, shooting free throws and generally taking it easy. No words were exchanged between Will and Bryce. Coach Hammett ignored both boys, except to instruct Bryce on a new inbounds play the team would use the next night.

With less than 24 hours until their first game in the Greenfield Tournament, the Bearcats were loose and ready to play, despite the unspoken turmoil in the locker room. It hadn't taken long for Ty to be accepted by the older players. He was contributing on the court, the main ingredient in becoming one of the guys.

Even Bryce was friendly to Ty.

When practice ended, Will caught a text message on his phone from Shelby: "Saw the bracket today. Tough first-round game for you guys. The coaches here make out the bracket. Looks like they're trying to keep our teams separate, send Baltic home quickly if they can."

"Yeah, I was thinking the same thing," Will responded. "From what I hear, the two best teams will be playing each other in the first round. Samuel Chester is supposed to be really good. Bus leaves here at 2:30 tomorrow. I'll try to say hello before the game. My parents are coming if you want to sit with them. They'd love to see you."

"Sure!" Shelby replied.

"See you then," Will said.

"OK … good luck!"

The Bearcats would need all the luck they could get. Samuel Chester Junior High, located a half hour south of Greenfield, had one of the biggest ninth-grade teams anyone had ever seen. Its front line players were all taller than 6-2 and they could all play. Cam will be in for a battle, Will thought, and the rest of the team will have to play extremely well just for Baltic to have a chance to win.

The only thing Samuel Chester didn't do well was defend the three-point shot. Coach Hammett pointed out that he'd scouted SC earlier in the season and, while the Bears had won by plenty, their opponent had scorched them from long range. Will took that as a good sign. He was probably the best three-point shooter on the team. Hopefully, that meant he'd have plenty of playing time.

He wouldn't be in the starting lineup, though. He and Ty grabbed the two spots closest to Coach Hammett as the game began. That was by design and the seats were typically reserved for the first substitutes to enter the game. By Will's assessment, it looked like Coach might give Ty an early call at point guard.

Will glanced across the arena and saw that Shelby had joined his parents in the stands. She caught his eye and sent a quick wave his way. Will smiled and threw his attention back to the game.

There was no secret to the Samuel Chester offense. The ball went inside the first five possessions and the Bears took

33

an 8-3 lead. After two more inside baskets and a pair of turnovers by Ian, Coach Hammett called timeout.

"Ty, in for Ian," he shouted. Ty tossed away his shooting shirt and headed to the scorer's table to check in. Ian, looking almost thankful for the relief, took a seat. Will stayed alert, expecting to also be sent into the game. But the call didn't come.

Ty ran the offense efficiently and knocked down a pair of jump shots in the final two minutes of the quarter. Samuel Chester led 14-9 at the first break. Ian was getting comfortable on the bench. Unfortunately, Will was still there with him.

It's only one quarter, Will reminded himself. Stay alert! He couldn't help but lift his eyes a bit and check Shelby's reaction to the game. Her hair was longer than last time he'd seen her in person, which had been nearly a month ago. Of course, he'd noticed it in the picture Cam had sent. But, that was a photo he was trying to forget.

Bryce scored inside and Will glanced nervously to the stands. Shelby was clapping for him and it unsettled Will. Of course, his parents were also clapping. At least he knew they were cheering for the team, though.

Midway through the second quarter, Cam was starting to get into the flow of the game. He had eight points already and, combined with Ty's efforts, was keeping Baltic in the game. It was still a struggle for him defensively, though, as he wasn't getting much help inside from either Jeffrey or Bryce.

With two minutes until the half and Baltic trailing 31-22, Coach Hammett turned to face Will on the bench. His eyes avoided Will, though.

"Ian, back in for Ty," he shouted.

Another turnover by Ian allowed Samuel Chester a quick basket and the Bears led 35-22 at the half. In the locker room, Will suddenly felt like so many of his teammates over the years. He'd never given much thought to the psyche of his friends who never actually got into a game. His rather simple theory was that if they weren't playing, maybe they should practice harder and get better.

He couldn't remember a game in his life that he hadn't played for an entire half, save the second half of his first varsity football game. He'd known why he wasn't playing then. Now, he was confused and angry at missing two quarters of action.

Especially with his girlfriend in the stands.

"Ty, you'll start the second half," Coach Hammett said as the team gathered to return to the floor. "It's junior high basketball, guys. Six-minute quarters go quickly. We have to make a run at them right now if we're going to get back into this game."

Ty and Cam continued to shine in the third quarter and Jeffrey began to make plays he didn't usually make. He scored inside twice and then stepped outside to hit a three-pointer, closing the SC lead to just three points heading into the final quarter.

Ian remained on the bench. It was becoming obvious to everyone he had just lost his starting spot to a seventh grader.

The teams traded baskets for most of the fourth quarter until Ty made a steal and dished to Cam for a layup. Cam was fouled on the shot and his free throw gave Baltic a 53-52 lead with just 14 seconds left.

Samuel Chester held the ball to take the game's final shot. When the clock hit five seconds, the ball floated inside to one of the Bears' taller players. Cam, making perhaps the play of his life, ignored the player's head fake and went straight up to block the shot. Ty picked up the loose ball and raced away from the crowd as the clock hit 0:00.

Will watched it all from the bench.

Chapter 7

He was still too angry to join in much of the celebration in the locker room after the team's biggest win of the season. Will tried to do just enough, though, that no one would notice how upset he was that he hadn't played.

While those around him slapped each other's hands and congratulated teammates on the win, Will dressed quickly and headed out the door. Closing the door behind him, he nearly bumped into Coach Hammett in the hallway.

"Come see me tomorrow before practice," Coach said. "We need to talk."

"Yes sir," Will said, barely breaking his stride as he headed off to find his parents. Will wasn't even certain he wanted to see Shelby at the moment. Of course he wanted to see her but he'd rarely been in this position. He'd never sat and watched his team win a game without him, when he was available to help them.

He didn't know what Coach Hammett wanted to talk about. He certainly didn't know why he hadn't played. Only two subs had made it into the game and he had been with the team barely a week, so maybe he didn't have a right to be mad.

His dad met him at the edge of the stands, heading down as Will was starting to climb the stairs.

"Hey, Mom and Shelby are right up there," Steve Stover said. "Is Ty out yet?"

"No sir. He's still in there," Will said matter-of-factly."

Sensing his oldest son's frustration, Steve took Will's arm and turned him around.

"Let's talk a second."

"Not really in the mood right now, Dad. And, I want to see Shelby. I haven't seen her in a month, you know," Will said. It wasn't often Will spoke in such harsh terms with his father.

"Give me a minute, OK?" Steve said. Will nodded.

"I know you're upset that you didn't play. I get that," he said. "You know what though, Will? It's not all about you. Your little brother just played the best game of his life. How about changing your attitude and enjoying his success? Would that be too much to ask?"

The lecture continued.

"Listen. It's still early in the season. You're still in football mode. This was a tight game all the way and maybe Coach didn't think you were quite ready for this yet," he said. "Hang in there and just be ready to play when he puts you in. And, keep working hard in practice. Right now, though, you need to give your brother his moment in the sun."

"OK," was all Will could manage. He knew his dad had never sat on a bench while his teammates proved they didn't need him. He turned again, eager to end the conversation.

"I mean it, Will," his father said. "Things aren't going to get better for you unless the attitude changes."

"Yes sir."

Will found his mom and Shelby. They gave him quick hugs and awkward congratulations. Will recognized the words because they were the same he used with teammates who rarely got to play. He'd used them many times without thinking how shallow they sounded.

"I'm hungry," Will said. "Are we going to stay or can we go to College Burger?"

The College Burger was semi-famous as the local hangout for Valley Tech students.

"I think we were going to hang around and watch some of the next game," Alicia said. Her motherly tone said that she understood Will's unhappiness and would do her best to alter the plans. "You guys play tomorrow night against the winner of this game."

"Well, I'd rather go eat. These two teams are horrible. We'll destroy either of them," Will said. "Well, our guys who get to play will destroy them."

Both Shelby and his mother ignored Will's whining.

39

"Let's wait for Ty. Your dad went to get him," Alicia said. "Oh, and try to be happy for him."

"Dad already warned me," Will said. He turned his attention to Shelby.

"So, how does it feel to date a guy who sits on the bench the whole game?"

"I'm good with it," Shelby said. "Doesn't sound like you are, though."

"I just can't figure out why Coach didn't let me play," Will said. "It's not like me playing, even for a few minutes, was going to get us beat."

"I don't know, Will. How about if we talk about something else? Do you realize we haven't seen each other in a month and this isn't exactly the reunion I had pictured?"

"Sorry," Will said. "It's just …"

"Seriously, Will," Shelby interrupted. "I get it. Can we move on?"

"Yeah. I'm starving, though. And, I don't really want to stay here," Will said.

"I, I, I, me, me, me …" Shelby mocked. "It's getting old, Will."

"Sorry."

Ty and Cam approached with Mr. Stover, who was reading a text on his phone.

"How about we all head over to College Burger?" Steve said, trying desperately to pretend it was his idea. "You guys must be starved. Shelby, can you come with us? We can take you home after if it's OK with your parents."

"Sure. Sounds good," she said. She gave Ty a playful pat on the head. "Great game, little guy! You too, Cam!"

Ouch, Will thought.

After ordering food, Will and Shelby found a table for two while the others sat together.

"So, tell me about school and all that," Will said.

"It's fine, I guess," Shelby said. "Classes are about the same as at Baltic. The kids seem to be a little more uppity. They *do* have a college and a mall here," she smirked.

She laughed at herself.

"Some of them are pretty nice, though. It's not too bad."

"Are you having to fend off the guys?" Will asked. He'd been wondering for several weeks now but didn't know how to ask the question.

"Hasn't really been a problem," Shelby said. "Most of the guys are either already dating someone or they know about you. You're quite well-known in Greenfield, Mr. Stover."

It was Will's turn to laugh. He had quarterbacked Baltic's varsity to two wins over the Greenfield Goblins in the fall. The second of those was for a state championship. Besides his dad owning one of the largest businesses in Greenfield, his family name was on one of the men's dormitories on the Valley Tech campus.

"I guess they do."

"It's just a little weird not getting to see you much," Shelby continued. "It's something we'll get used to, I guess. At least I'll get to see you a few times this week."

"Hopefully, you'll actually get to see me play a little at some point," Will said.

"Stop!" It was a playful voice from Shelby but she wasn't smiling when she said it. Will made a mental note that Shelby wasn't big on guys having drama.

He changed the subject.

"Everything's about the same at school," Will said. "Except you not being there, I mean. How's your dad's work going?"

Shelby's dad had taken over her grandfather's insurance company in Greenfield when her grandfather retired, prompting the move.

"Seems like it's going fine," she said. "I've been working for him a couple days a week in the office. I think it's fun. It's interesting."

42

"Insurance is interesting?" Will asked with a smirk.

"If you make it interesting, it is," she said.

Steve and Alicia signaled to the two that it was time to leave. They took Shelby home, where an awkward "they're-watching-us" hug took place between Will and Shelby.

"See you tomorrow," Will said.

"I like the sound of that!" Shelby said and smiled before disappearing inside.

Chapter 8

Coach Hammett's office door was open when Will stopped by a half hour before practice was to begin.

"Hey, Coach," Will said. "You wanted to see me?"

"Yeah. Grab a seat, Will," he said.

Will studied the walls. He'd only been in Coach Hammett's office a few times and never for more than a minute or two. Photos of the coach from his college days were displayed proudly. He'd played basketball at Valley Tech a few years before Steve Stover had arrived there on a football scholarship. The school's most recent basketball state championship trophy, from three years earlier, sat on a filing cabinet. Will knew it was supposed to be in the school's trophy case in the lobby of the gymnasium but it hadn't made it there yet.

A team picture from each of the 24 varsity teams he'd coached at Baltic hung neatly on the wall, in four rows of six. The next one would require additional math, Will thought. Coach Hammett's state title year already a distant memory, this year's varsity squad was off to a rough start, having won just four of its first ten games.

Will waited for Coach Hammett to open the conversation. Will was still angry, though he'd decided he wasn't going to let anyone else know that. Whatever frustration he had would be rechanneled into extra energy for the practice court. If

Coach was going to keep him off the court in games that mattered, Will would treat his practices as games.

"I'm disappointed in you," Coach Hammett said. Those weren't the words Will imagined he would hear. He quickly remembered Sunday's scrimmage and the look Coach had given him after calling him and Bryce off the court.

Will wasn't sure how to respond, so he remained silent.

"I expect things like that from Bryce," Coach Hammett said quietly. "But I expect you to be above a brawl on my practice court."

Will wanted to shout that he hadn't started it, that he was only standing up for himself. He wanted to demand to know why Coach Hammett had kept him out of the game the night before.

But he sat silently.

"I don't know exactly what's going on between the two of you. Frankly, I don't care," Coach Hammett said. "It's not my responsibility to decipher every little disagreement my players have. My problem, though, is that you didn't handle that the way you normally handle things around here."

Will nodded but didn't speak.

"Listen, Will," Coach continued. "I know what you went through at the beginning of football season. I talk with Coach Peterson and Coach Bishop every day. It's not that big of a school. I also know there was some resentment from the other ninth graders over you moving up in football.

"And I know you handled it well all the way through," he said.

Will nodded again.

"So, I have to ask. Why are you disrupting my practice with whatever this is between you and Bryce?"

Again, Will wanted to shout that he was just defending himself. Deep down, though, he knew better.

"I don't know," Will said. "He just kind of gets to me. I haven't done anything to him but we've never gotten along."

"Is this over a girl? The type of thing I witnessed out there is usually over a girl. I've been coaching high school and junior high kids a long time, Will. Trust me. It's usually over a girl."

"Sort of, I guess," Will admitted.

Coach Hammett grinned as if patting himself on the back for his insight.

"Thought so," he said. Then, he turned serious again.

"Will, this *might* be the best junior high team I've ever coached. Obviously, it's a little early to say that. We'll have to see how the season plays out and then that'll be for others to decide, if they wish. But, I'm telling you, we have a real chance to go undefeated this year. That's never happened in junior high basketball at Baltic. At least not since I've been here."

"Yes sir," Will said, nodding. He was beginning to understand where this was going. Still, he wanted to ask what his role might be.

"I can't stop every little bit of teenage jealousy or whatever it is, that comes up out here," Coach Hammett said. "To be honest, after 24 years, I'm quite tired of it all. Makes a guy want to go coach at an all-boys school where these distractions don't show up every year. What I'm not going to allow, though, is for two of my better players to disrupt what we've got going here."

"Is this why I didn't play last night?"

Will almost couldn't believe he'd asked the question but immediately felt better that he had. He'd never questioned a coach before, especially about playing time.

"Yep. I thought that would be the best way to get a message through to you," Coach Hammett said.

"Then why did Bryce get to play?" Will interrupted. He had pretty much thrown caution to the wind at this point, so why not press on?

"Because of what I told you before," Coach said. "I expect this kind of thing out of Bryce. Bryce has been here for a month and he's been working hard. It seems to me that it's up to you to come out here and reestablish yourself with your

47

classmates. Don't you think it would be asking a little much for them to all bend over backwards to welcome you back with open arms? They feel like you abandoned them in football. Now, I know and you know that you had no control over that. But, Will, these are kids who are 12, 13, 14 years old. If you were one of them, I think you'd understand how they feel."

"I hated missing that game, Coach," Will said. "I've never had to sit and watch my team for that long before."

"Good. Mission accomplished then," Coach Hammett said. "Get your head back on right and get ready to play. We have two more games, hopefully, at Greenfield. Then, we have the rest of the season to deal with. You're going to make us a better team. I know that. But, I thought last night was important. Sometimes you have to realize you need a team more than a team needs you."

"Yes sir," Will said.

"No real practice today, just free throws," Coach Hammett said. "Go get ready, though. I think I hear the others coming in."

Chapter 9

Will forced a smile and picked up a loose basketball then joined half his team around the free throw line. The other half was gathered at the opposite basket. The object was for each player to shoot five free throws and rotate. Each player needed to sink 50 before he was allowed to leave.

Time to make a little statement, Will thought.

When his turn came, he doubled his normal focus on the front of the rim. He took his customary four dribbles and lofted the ball easily into the net. He repeated the motion four more times and moved on. At this rate, Will thought, I'll be the first one gone.

Every other player missed at least once on their first five attempts. Will knew because he kept track of such things. It's a competition and he wasn't going to lose, he told himself. He also knew this was a drill that few other players took seriously, even Ty. Will's little brother was the second-best free throw shooter on the team. The brothers had been having free throw shooting contests since they were old enough to reach the rim with a basketball.

It was common to make friendly wagers on their backyard shooting contests: loser makes the winner's bed for a week; loser takes the winner's turn clearing the dinner table. Will had once forced his little brother to mow the lawn every Saturday for a month. That was the one that made Ty stop betting with his brother.

After seven trips to the line, Will was a perfect 35-of-35 and his teammates were beginning to notice. Time to have a little fun with it, Will thought. The shooting drill was unsupervised as Coach Hammett watched half-heartedly from a seat in the stands.

Stepping back to the line, all chatter stopped as players turned to watch. Even the teammates on the other line had heard about Will's perfection and were halting their own shooting to watch Will. He took his four dribbles and stared at the rim. With all eyes on him, he suddenly switched the ball to his left hand and, without missing a beat, sent the ball soaring toward the rim. Teammates held their breath as they watched the flight of the ball.

Swish.

A low cheer and a couple laughs escaped the group. Coach Hammett rolled his eyes from afar and picked up a newspaper.

Enough showboating, Will thought to himself. He switched the next ball back to his right hand and quickly finished netting the last four. He finally missed on the 49th shot and was forced to wait through another rotation before finishing.

Still, he'd reminded everyone he was the best shooter on the team.

Will's free throw shooting exhibition might have been a sign of things to come. Playing against Winston Junior High in the tournament semifinals that night, Will checked into the game midway through the first quarter. Ty, who was now starting at the point guard spot, repeatedly penetrated deep into the lane before turning and finding Will spotted up behind the three-point line. Will drilled the first seven shots he put into the air, all from behind the arc. At the half, Baltic led Winston, 37-14.

Substitutes played almost the entire second half and still maintained the advantage over the helpless Winston squad. The easy win verified the suspicions that Greenfield coaches had doctored the brackets, hoping to send the Bearcats home after the first round.

Cam had another good game, scoring 15 points. As he reminded Will on the bench during the fourth quarter, "I'd better make the all-tournament team this year."

"Big game tomorrow night," Will reminded his friend. "Let's win the tournament first."

Shelby was glad to see Will in a better mood after his unmatched shooting performance in the first half. They sat together and watched most of the Greenfield game that followed. Just before halftime, Bryce walked by the couple. As if spotting Shelby for the first time in weeks, he leaned over and offered a quick hug. He didn't speak to or look at Will.

"Good game tonight, Bryce," Will said.

The compliment seemed to catch his rival off guard. Bryce stammered before sending a half glare in Will's direction.

"Yeah, thanks. You, too," he said before walking away quickly.

"That was nice of you," Shelby said, patting Will on the knee.

"Just talking to a teammate," Will said with a grin.

"Well, I'm more proud of you for that than I was for the seven 3-pointers!" she said, smiling. "You're going to make a mature adult one day, Will Stover."

"Hey, I almost forgot," Will said hurriedly. "My parents didn't make it over for the game tonight – I guess you know that by now. They wanted me to see if you and your parents could come to dinner Friday night. There's a high school game after that, if you want to go."

"I'll ask. That sounds great, though. I think they want to watch you play tomorrow night in the finals. Maybe they can talk about it then," Shelby said.

"OK. I gotta run. Coach just texted. Bus is about to leave," Will said.

He gave Shelby a quick hug and turned to leave.

"See you tomorrow," he said.

The tournament final was much less dramatic than expected. Once Baltic beat Samuel Chester in the opening round, it was a foregone conclusion the Bearcats would win the Greenfield Tournament for the first time in 10 years.

The host team wasn't bad but it was no match for Baltic, which improved to 8-0 on the season. Will didn't start the game but was the first substitute in. He drained five more three-point shots, giving him 12 in just two tournament games. Cam controlled the game, scoring 21 points and gathering 13 rebounds.

Not only was Cam named to the all-tournament team, he was chosen as the tournament's most valuable player. Because they'd won the tournament, four players from the Bearcats' squad were named to the team. Bryce was something of a surprise pick, though he'd played a solid three games. Ty was the only seventh grader chosen, but that wasn't a surprise. He'd had just five turnovers in the three games and had shot the ball well when the team needed him to score.

Evidently, Will's three-point barrage was too much to ignore as he was the fourth Baltic player selected. Coach Hammett didn't acknowledge the honors, instead focusing on the team's eight-game win streak and tournament title. The trophy was a traveling trophy, meaning the winning school had the right to keep it until the next year's event. It had been a long time since Coach Hammett had been able to take home the award.

He had cleared a spot on a filing cabinet earlier that day.

Chapter 10

Two conference games were sandwiched between the Greenfield Tournament and the beginning of the annual county tournament for the Baltic Bearcats. Both proved to be easy wins for the Bearcats, pushing their record to 10-0.

Will had become the team's designated sixth man, coming off the bench to provide an offensive spark. The way things had been going, there was little need for further spark. The recent games had nearly been decided by the time Will entered them. That wasn't by design ... Baltic's team was just that much better than the opposition's.

Ty continued to play well and Ian was there to give him a breather now and then. With junior high games lasting just 24 minutes, though, Ty rarely needed to leave the game. Ian, who had started for the team the previous season, was relegated to mop-up duty.

Bryce was still giving Will the cold shoulder but was amicable, getting along just enough to get things done on the court and not negatively affect the team. After hearing Coach Hammett's bold predictions about the team, Will had totally bought in, realizing there was something special about this group.

Jeffrey had been playing better, with only an occasional glimpse of the inconsistent play. Luke's shooting ability still wasn't on par with Will's but Coach Hammett saw no need to tinker with the chemistry of an unbeaten team.

Cam seemingly got better each day. Much like he did as a receiver in football, his work ethic was tremendous, routinely staying after practice or arriving early to get in more shots or to work with the school's rebounding machine.

Will had come to terms with his new role on the team. At least until they lost a game, any argument he'd make would only cause a distraction.

The county tournament was set to begin the following Monday. Will and his parents were headed to Greenfield on Saturday for a return dinner with the Sparks. Shelby and her parents had been back in town the previous weekend and the parents of the lovebirds got along wonderfully. Will's mom, Alicia, was going to Greenfield earlier in the day to spend the afternoon shopping with Shelby's mom.

Ty was going along, hoping for another chance meeting with Shelby's cousin Lydia.

"She's cute. She can't help it and I can't either," he told Will on the way to Greenfield.

Thanks to the Greenfield Tournament, Will had had gotten to see Shelby quite a bit in the past couple of weeks. While he hoped the fledgling friendship between the sets of parents worked out, he also worried that it put a little extra pressure on Shelby and him.

The families enjoyed dinner, told embarrassing stories about their respective children, and then sat around a fire in the Sparks' backyard. Glancing at his watch several hours later and not wanting to wear thin their welcome, Steve stood and stretched.

"We've got to get going, guys," he said. "This has been a lot of fun, though. It's our turn to entertain next. I'll let Alicia put that together. She's the social director in the family."

The families laughed and said their goodbyes.

Forty-five minutes later, the Stovers were met with a rude welcome at home in Baltic. Before they pulled into the driveway, they immediately noticed a "For Sale" sign on the front lawn. Steve stopped the car, jumped out and pulled the stakes out of the ground. He motioned for his wife to open the garage door and he flipped the sign inside.

That was about the time Ty noticed the front door. Rotten eggs had been tossed against the brick front, all the way up to the second floor balcony that led to Chelsea's bedroom. The eggs were everywhere and it appeared it had been done several hours earlier. The smell was awful.

"Will, Ty … get the water hose and get that off the house," Steve said. "Alicia, go make sure Chelsea is OK. She's been home all night, hasn't she?"

"Yes," Alicia muttered in anger as she ran into the house yelling Chelsea's name.

She found Chelsea sitting in the floor in her bedroom, almost hiding between her bed and an outside wall. She'd heard the commotion and had peeked outside. There were two boys, she said, but she couldn't make out their faces. She hadn't known if they knew she was home and had wanted to frighten her.

If they had, it certainly worked. The boys threw eggs and something that sounded more destructive, though she had been too afraid to go outside to check the damage.

"DAD!"

Steve had joined Alicia inside to check on Chelsea. He ran back down the stairs, meeting Ty at the back door.

"You're not going to like this," Ty said, out of breath. "It's the basketball court. Spray paint. And the backboards are both shattered. It isn't pretty."

Steve walked toward the near goal and began picking up the larger pieces of glass while he looked around the yard for further signs of vandalism. There were a few words painted on the court that would need immediate attention. The cleaner message simply read, "Superstar".

Clearly, it was aimed at Will. And Will had a pretty good idea who was behind the mess.

His dad glanced his direction, almost reading his mind, and said, "Don't even think about it, son. We have no idea who did this. First thing in the morning, I'll let the police know. I'm just thankful your sister is OK. She was scared to death up there."

Will went inside to gather garbage bags for the glass that was strewn all over the court. Chelsea and his mother were in the kitchen. Chelsea repeated the story for Will. He paused when she mentioned seeing two boys.

"Any idea who they were?" he asked. He told his mom and sister about the damage in the back.

"No. I got away from the window pretty quickly. I didn't want them to see me or know that I'd seen them. Anyone who would do all this has to be pretty mean," Chelsea said. "I didn't recognize them. We'll probably never know who did it."

"I've got a pretty good idea," Will said.

"Who?" his mother asked sharply.

"It doesn't matter right now, but I've got an idea," Will said. "I'm not sure who the second one would be, though. I'll be back. I've got to get back and help them clean this up."

The next day, a police officer walked into the back yard while Will, Ty and his father were cleaning. Shaking his head, the officer said, "Someone did a number here, didn't they? Both basketball goals? Those backboards aren't cheap. I've priced them before. Wanted to get one for my son when we moved here several years ago."

It was then that Will recognized the man, though neither his father nor Ty had yet. He glanced at the badge and saw the word, "Locklin".

This is going to get interesting, Will thought.

When Mr. Stover finally made the connection, he quickly shook hands with the officer.

"I'm sorry. I knew you looked familiar, but I had no idea you were a police officer," Steve said. "Yes, whoever it was certainly did a number back here. I don't mind replacing the things. That's not that big of a deal. My daughter was home alone, though, and they really frightened her."

"They? Did she see someone?" Officer Locklin asked.

"She said she looked out a window when it first started … the eggs on the front of the house," Steve said. "She said she saw two guys but couldn't identify them, even with the lights on in front."

"This is pretty rare in this neighborhood," Officer Locklin said. "I can't remember the last call we had for something like this. What does that say over there?" He was staring at the "superstar" written on the court. Of course, Will had picked it out immediately as Bryce's pet name for him.

"It says 'Superstar' ", Will said, hoping this might ring a bell for the officer. Maybe he'd heard mention of it at home at some point.

"That's odd. Any idea what that's supposed to mean?" he asked.

"No idea," Steve said.

"No sir. No idea at all," Will said, walking back inside.

Chapter 11

Will was waiting just inside the front entrance to the school when Bryce made his way through the door. Most days, Bryce and his sister Maggie rode to school with Kyle, who had dated Maggie for almost a year. Will angrily grabbed Bryce by the jacket and pulled him through the door and into an empty classroom.

It took Bryce a second to realize what was going on. Kyle was just behind the two, standing in the doorway. Maggie abandoned the excitement and made her way to her first class.

Bryce shook himself free of Will's hold and turned with a balled fist. Before he could take action, though, Kyle stepped into the room and stood between the rivals.

"What's going on here, Will? What are you doing?" Kyle asked.

"I don't think he knows what he's doing because he's about to make a huge mistake," Bryce interjected. "Don't ever put your hands on me again. If you've got a problem with me, then let's settle it. Don't ever grab me like that again, though."

Will hadn't counted on Kyle being present and now he was slightly relieved that a calm head was in the midst of the altercation.

"Bryce knows what this is about," Will said, spitting out the words. "It's not that I have a problem with you, Bryce. It's you that has the problem."

Kyle had a hand in each boy's chest, keeping them as far apart as possible without seeming threatening. Will wondered where Kyle's allegiance might lie if he was forced to choose. He knew Kyle wouldn't go against his girlfriend's little brother. He'd been nicer than most during the fall, though, especially when Will was struggling in football.

"I don't know what this is all about, Will, but I think you guys need to get on to class," Kyle said. "Picking a fight right here ... inside the building ... not your brightest move, Will."

It was then that Will noticed a quick smirk on Kyle's face. It vanished as quickly as it had appeared but Will had seen it.

The realization hit Will like a ton of bricks. It had never occurred to him that the other person who might be upset with him – enough to vandalize his home – would be Kyle. It had never crossed his mind, though, because he wouldn't have believed it.

But then, he saw the smirk again.

"What's your problem with Bryce, anyway?"

"Like I said, he knows what it's about," Will said, still angry but regaining a little control. He looked past Kyle into Bryce's eyes.

"Your dad came to my house," Will said. "He asked what the 'superstar' meant."

Bryce's face lightened several shades.

"I don't know what you're talking about," he said. "My dad goes to a lot of places. It's his job. When he goes to someone's house, it's usually a domestic dispute or something like that. Everything good with your folks, Will?"

Bryce ended the sarcasm with a smirk of his own.

"It's going to be pretty embarrassing when he finds out it was his son who did that to our house," Will said. "And, it's going to be a lot of fun to let him know."

"You've got no proof," Bryce said, still smirking yet visibly shaken by the threat.

Coach Bishop, nearing the door where Will had begun the scene, heard the voices and glanced into the classroom.

"Everything OK in here, guys?"

Kyle took the lead.

"Sure, Coach. We're all about to head to class. Just had to settle a couple of things in here," he said.

"Well, you guys don't need to be standing around in an empty classroom. It doesn't look good. Now, get to class," Coach Bishop said before exiting.

Bryce was almost to the hallway when Will spoke again.

"Bryce, you're not going to get away with this," Will said. "You did a lot of damage. It's going to cost someone some money."

"You guys had the money to put all your fancy stuff up in the first place; you've got money to put it back," Bryce said and stormed down the hallway.

Kyle turned back to face Will.

"Hey, I know Bryce can be a little hothead but he wouldn't have done anything like trashing your house," Kyle said. "And you've seen him throw. I don't think he could even hit your house with an egg."

"Never mentioned anything about eggs, Kyle," Will said without looking at Kyle as he brushed past him into the hallway. Turning back, he added, "and we know there were two guys there."

Kyle didn't respond.

Will had learned his lesson about creating controversy within the basketball team. He certainly wasn't planning to add to his earlier punishment and managed to avoid Bryce the rest of the school day. Only in practice did he interact with him and then only enough to keep the peace.

He'd decided to wait before telling his father anything about the incident at home. The only real purpose it would serve now would be revenge. The Bearcats were still unbeaten and, after Will's previous talk with Coach Hammett, he wasn't going to risk getting Bryce into trouble now.

Baltic opened the county tournament that night with an easy win over Pleasant View. Will knocked down six 3-point shots in the first half. He only played a quarter but his shooting expedition, along with 12 points from Cam, had the Bearcats in complete control by halftime.

Baltic, which was serving as the host for this year's tournament, was responsible for its players helping out around the gym once their game ended. Will, Cam and Ty spent the rest of the evening working the concession stand, bagging popcorn and pouring drinks for fans. The three of them knew this might be the most excitement the county tournament would provide. No other junior high team in the county could come close to matching the Bearcats.

The next night saw Baltic take an even easier victory. Coach Hammett cleared the bench before the first half was over, running wide-eyed seventh graders into the game as early as the second quarter. Ty, being a seventh grader himself, was left on the floor to keep the chaos to a minimum. By the time it was over, the Bearcats were simply trying to remain interested.

They were still unbeaten at 12-0 and sitting in the finals of the county tournament .

Chapter 12

The next day's practice brought more of a challenge than the team had seen all year. Figuring his junior high players might be getting a little full of themselves – and because of the off day in the tournament schedule – Coach Hammett brought the senior high team together with the juniors for a scrimmage.

The varsity Bearcats were still struggling through a mediocre season. They'd managed a few decent wins but couldn't string many together, a growing frustration for the veteran coach.

"The varsity needs a little confidence boost and I've got a junior high team that thinks it can beat the Duke Blue Devils," Coach Hammett told a teacher in the hallway earlier in the day. "Maybe this will do both of them some good."

This could go very badly, Will thought to himself as he watched the opening tip from the bench. Though his team was much younger and weaker, this would be no cakewalk for the varsity. He was itching to get on the court. He'd watched almost all of the big team's games this year and, without realizing he'd ever need it, had a scouting report that would have made Coach proud.

"They haven't stopped teams shooting the three-pointer all year," he told Cam before the teams took the court. "They know you're the best player we have and they're going to collapse on you every time you touch the ball, if they even let you touch it. If you get it inside, look for the shooters. They'll be open."

As if sensing how timid the junior high bunch was to begin the game, the varsity Bearcats took advantage, moving the ball inside against Cam and scoring easily the first three times down the court. They pressed the juniors the entire court, forcing Ty into two turnovers before Coach Hammett – sitting with the junior high team – called timeout.

"Settle down, guys. They think you're afraid of them and right now, it looks like you are," Coach Hammett said. "The reason I wanted to do this is to make you guys better. Sooner or later, we're going to face a team that gives you a lot of pressure. I promise you we'll face another team like Samuel Chester this year ... probably a better one. Just settle down and take care of the ball."

The talk seemed to help as Ty regained control of the offense. Coach Hammett had sent Will into the game after the timeout and Cam followed his earlier instructions perfectly. Feeling a double-team coming after receiving a pass from Ty, he immediately whipped the ball back out to Will, who calmly sank a three-pointer.

Ty and Will took turns burning the varsity squad with long-range shots until the defense finally stretched itself enough to guard them on the perimeter. Once they did, though, Cam had room to work inside. He scored on consecutive trips down the floor before Coach called another timeout. Now, he was sitting on the varsity bench.

Treating it like an actual game, Coach Hammett had the teams play four full eight-minute quarters, the equivalent of a varsity game. Late in the third quarter, Ty was beginning to wear down. He'd already played longer than a junior high game typically lasts, and the varsity team had applied full-court pressure almost the entire time.

Slowly, the varsity squad took control of the game. Cam, with little help from Bryce on the inside, was outmanned by the bigger opponents. Coach Hammett called a halt to the action midway through the final quarter.

It had been a more than respectable showing by the junior high team. Once it was over and the varsity players relaxed, they congratulated the younger guys on a good effort. Coach Hammett had put his older team into an unenviable position. If they'd lost, they would have never heard the end of it. By winning, they simply did what they were supposed to do.

Coach Hammett's tactic really hadn't worked on the junior high team, though. The intention was for the varsity to take the younger boys down a couple notches. Instead, the junior Bearcats walked out of the gym thinking they were even better than before.

And that's when the trouble began.

Not expecting much of a challenge from Bay Central the next night in the county tournament finals, the junior Baltic team looked sluggish and out of the game mentally. Trailing 8-0 in the first two minutes of the game, Coach Hammett called a timeout.

"This team is nowhere near as good as you are," he began. "But … they're better than you think they are, so you'd better get it together and start playing. Trust me, guys. If you lose to this team, you're going to remember this night for a long time. And, it won't be for the right reasons. Get it straightened out right now, before it's too late."

The talk did nothing to motivate the Bearcats.

Three mid-range jump shots by Luke kept Baltic in the game. The Bearcats were getting nothing from Cam, who was routinely being double-teamed now. At the half, Baltic trailed 21-12. Will had played briefly in the second quarter but missed his first three shots and Coach had sent Luke back into the game.

The third quarter was more of the same as Bay Central extended its lead to 33-20. Just six minutes of basketball remained and the Bearcats' unblemished record was on the line. Will couldn't help but remember Coach Hammett's words just a couple of weeks earlier.

"This might be the best junior high team I've ever coached." That's what he had said. Well, the Bearcats certainly didn't look like it tonight.

Will checked into the game for Luke, who had gone cold shooting the ball. For the most part, Bay Central had played a zone defense and sagged in on Cam, all but making him a non-factor in the game. When Luke got hot in the first half, the Bruins had sent one player to chase him around the court. It resembled a box-and-one. When Luke cooled, though, Bay Central had abandoned the junk defense.

Will was expecting the Bruins to go back to the special defense when he checked into the game. The Bay Central coach was a Baltic alum who was close friends with Coach Hammett and had once been a Bearcat himself. He knew all about Will's shooting ability, even if he hadn't seen it yet tonight.

Will guessed correctly. As soon as the ball crossed midcourt, one defender located Will on the perimeter and left the zone defense. After 10 seconds, Will realized that if he went to the concession stand for a snow cone, this defender would be standing there. He might even offer to pay.

With the three-point shot in play, Will knew his team was only down a little more than four possessions. The problem, he knew, was the short six-minute quarters in junior high games. There wouldn't be much time.

He ran the defender into two teammates before freeing himself for a shot. Ty found him moving to the corner and met him there with a pass. Will launched the shot and it found the net, cutting the lead to 10.

Cam suddenly felt the urgency of the situation and toughened inside. He blocked a shot, recovered it and hit Will with a baseball pass. Flying up the right sideline with one Bay Central player between him and the goal, Will suddenly applied the brakes and launched a 22-footer. Surprised, the defender could do nothing but turn and retrieve the ball as it fell through the net.

Another stop by the Baltic defense, this a steal by Bryce, resulted in a driving layup by Ty that cut the lead to 33-28 with 2:04 showing on the clock. Will then stole the inbounds pass and dished to Cam for an easy score.

Bay Central called timeout with 1:39 left. The Baltic fans, who normally wouldn't fill the gym for a junior high game, came to its feet cheering the Bearcats' run.

"Just keep the pressure on them," Coach Hammett said during the timeout. "They're trying to fold up, guys. Give them the chance. Let's get another stop down here and get the ball back."

The Bruins decided to take the air out of the ball, or at least attempt it. Baltic let Bay Central's guards toss the ball back and forth for nearly a minute before extending the defense and forcing the issue. A quick pass to the wing slipped off the fingertips of a Bruin and into the stands.

Ty took the inbounds pass and darted through the stunned Bay Central defense, which was expecting another three-point attempt by Will. The layup cut the lead to a single point. Will fouled a Bruin on the inbounds and the teams walked to the other end of the floor for a one-and-one.

The Bay Central player dropped the first shot through for a 34-32 lead and then missed the second. Cam grabbed the rebound and handed it to Ty. With 12 seconds left, Ty delivered a pass to Will, who faked a three-pointer and watched as the defender flew up for a block. Will easily dribbled by him and into the lane. The Bay Central post player came at Will quickly. Just before he got there, Will floated the ball toward the rim. It fell through the net as the player crashed into Will, sending him flying into the basket support.

The referee's whistle blew for a foul. He looked to the scorer's table and saw the official signal that the basket would also count.

Just one second remained on the clock as Will took a deep breath and stepped to the free throw line. His bucket had tied the game. Now, he could win it. Four dribbles. He focused on the front of the iron cylinder. He'd done it 10,000 times in his back yard.

The ball fell cleanly through the net.

The desperation heave at the buzzer wasn't close for the Bruins and Baltic's perfect season continued.

Chapter 13

With the county tournament behind them, the Bearcats turned their attention back to the conference schedule. Coach Hammett gave the team the weekend off with the warning: "You've had your wakeup call. You played an average team and played horribly ... and still found a way to win. That's the sign of a good team ... when you aren't playing your best but you still manage to get a victory. Now, rest up and let's get back to work Monday."

The Stovers set out for Greenfield early Saturday morning. Chelsea again found better things to do but Cam took her seat, as was his custom. The plan for the day was shopping for the adults and a day hanging out on the Valley Tech campus for Will, Ty and Cam.

The campus was like a second home for Will and Ty. Their parents began taking their children to Valley Tech long before either of the boys could walk. Their home and family photo albums were plastered with pictures of their three children at various points on the campus.

Chelsea was old enough to remember being present for the ceremony on the Valley Tech campus when the newest men's dormitory was named after her father. Will and Ty remembered it through photos. Chelsea had already been accepted at the school for the fall semester, something that had really been decided many years before. It was assumed that Will and Ty would follow their sister there.

It was a relatively small college and its athletic teams competed in Division II, a step down from most of the big-name schools in both enrollment and prestige. Athletic prestige, anyway. It had really been a fluke that Steve or Alicia Stover found themselves as students there some 20 years earlier. Alicia had grown up several hours north of Greenfield and attended on an academic scholarship while Steve, a Baltic native, had chosen Valley Tech over many other schools. He had been recruited primarily for baseball but the coaches at Valley Tech had been willing to let him play football as well.

The boys were sitting together in the student center, the gathering place for those living on campus, when Coach Pettitt walked in. Frank Pettitt had been the head football coach at Valley Tech for almost 30 years and had coached Steve years before. He immediately recognized Will and Ty and made his way over.

"Hello boys," he said with a big smile and an extended hand. "What brings you to campus today? You guys just here to look for girls?"

Coach Pettitt laughed at himself.

"No sir," Will said, shaking the coach's hand. "We're going to the basketball game tonight. Mom and Dad are out shopping. They'll be around later."

"Ty, are you ever going to grow, son?" It was a running joke Coach Pettitt had with Ty. He'd been asking the same question since Ty was four years old. Coach had, in fact, been at the hospital when each of the Stover boys had been born.

He would have been there for Chelsea's too but Alicia had gone to the hospital on a game day during the football season. On that day, he had called instead.

Ty blushed.

"I hope so, Coach," he said.

Cam, not one to be ignored and feeling like his introduction might not come, decided to take up his own cause.

"Hi Coach. It's good to meet you. I'm Cam Show."

"Aren't you a wide receiver on the junior high team? I've seen you at most of our home games."

Cam beamed that he had been recognized by the legendary coach. It really hadn't mattered that Cam was Will's best friend; Coach Pettitt likely knew the rosters of every high school team in the state.

"Franklin State tonight, isn't it? Coach asked, turning back to Will. "You picked a good one to see. Your dad care anything at all about basketball yet?"

"He tries to act interested, but not really," Will said.

"I don't guess I've talked to you since the football season ended. Congratulations. I saw most of the championship game. You guys had a really nice team," he said then looked back to Cam and Ty. "I hear you guys had a great season as well.

"Those magical seasons don't come along often," he added. "Enjoy it when it happens."

"Yes sir," all three managed to say as one.

"How's your basketball season going?" Coach asked. It was becoming obvious he wasn't in a hurry to get wherever he was going.

"Pretty good," Will said. "We haven't lost any. Cam and Ty are both starting for us."

"As a seventh grader?" Coach asked, glancing quickly back in Ty's direction.

"Yes sir," Ty said proudly. "And Cam's having a great year. I think Coach Spencer might need to start talking to him."

Coach Pettitt chuckled as Cam gave Ty a playful punch in the arm.

"Sounds like things are good in Baltic," he said. "You guys enjoy your time on campus and tell your folks I'll find them at the game tonight."

"OK. Bye, Coach," Will said.

Cam and Ty excused themselves. Cam wanted to be in the arena when the Valley Tech Mustangs arrived to get in some pre-game shooting. He was really hoping Coach Spencer might stop by for a quick hello. Will stayed behind as he was expecting Shelby any minute. She'd spent the morning working at her father's office, helping him catch up on paperwork. She was supposed to meet Will at noon and walk to College Burger for lunch.

At 12:15, his phone buzzed. The text from Shelby made his stomach growl: "Still at the office. Give me a half hour. Sorry!"

Tell that to my stomach, Will thought. Instead he quickly typed, "No problem. See you then."

Chapter 14

Shelby, wearing the Valley Tech sweatshirt Will had bought her for Christmas, looked as cute as any girl could look in a sweatshirt. Alicia had insisted he pick out something different, something a bit more elegant, she called it. Claiming he had no clue what girls liked to wear, Alicia had taken command of the rest of the gift buying, giving Will full credit, of course.

"I heard what happened at your house," Shelby said.

Will had made a point not to mention it to her. He was still certain he wouldn't mention the culprit's names to his parents, at least not now. He also hadn't mentioned it to Shelby.

"How'd you hear?" he asked.

"Bryce called me last night," Shelby said quietly.

"What!"

"Lower your voice, please," Shelby said with a serious look. "We're on a college campus. Let's at least act like adults."

"What do you mean, he called you?" Will asked.

"Yeah. I'm not exactly sure why. He didn't really say. Anyway, we starting talking and he said you tried to start a fight with him. Really, Will? That doesn't sound like something you'd do."

"Did he mention he's the one ... well, one of the ones ... who was at my house?"

"He said you're convinced it was him," Shelby said. "I really don't think he would do that, Will. I know you guys don't get along ... but that's really a stretch, isn't it?"

"He wrote 'Superstar' on the basketball court, Shelby," Will said.

"Oh."

"That's not all," Will said. "I know who the other one was."

"The other one?"

"Yes. Chelsea was at home when it happened. She saw two guys," Will said. "She didn't recognize them, though."

"Who was it?"

"Kyle," Will said, still shocked that it was true.

"Oh, Will ... there's no possible way. He wouldn't do something like that," Shelby said. "What makes you say that, anyway?"

"He dates Bryce's sister," Will began before Shelby cut him off.

"That's your reasoning?" Shelby said.

"That's not all. I just know they were together," Will said. "Believe me ... it surprised me, too. I know it was him, though.

When I talked to Bryce, it was like they were trying to cover for each other. And Kyle said a little too much."

"What'd he say?" Shelby asked.

"He knew they threw eggs," Will said.

"It's a small town, Will," Shelby said. "Everyone in Baltic probably knew someone egged your house before you guys even got home."

"But when I called him on it, he had a look on his face like I'd just busted him," Will said. "I really don't want to believe it, either. I thought a lot of the guy. But, I'm sure it was him."

"Have you told your parents that?" Shelby asked.

"Not yet. I'm going to wait until the season is over," Will said.

"Just make sure you're absolutely positive before you accuse someone of something like that, Will," she said.

"I will."

The two walked back to campus and hung out in the bookstore, waiting for Cam and Ty to join them. Will had already checked in with his mother twice since his parents had dropped them off, one of the rules of letting the boys stay on campus on their own.

"Guess where I'm going to college?"

Cam bolted through the bookstore's front entry. He was almost singing.

"I said … guess where I'm going to college?"

"What are you talking about?" Will asked.

Cam gave Shelby a quick hug, and then grabbed a hooded sweatshirt off a rack.

"Coach Spencer practically just offered me a scholarship," Cam squealed in a voice that sounded more like Shelby's than his own.

Ty, two steps behind Cam and facing Will and Shelby, slowly shook his head no at them.

"Well, he didn't exactly offer a scholarship, but he came pretty close," Cam said.

"What he actually said," Ty interrupted, "was that the coaches would have to 'keep an eye' on you over the next few years. I don't think they've assigned you a dorm room yet."

Everyone, including Cam, laughed.

"We could be teammates in college," he said excitedly to Will. "Except in different sports, I mean."

"That doesn't even make sense," Will said.

At that moment, someone approached Will from behind. Before he could move, two arms were wrapped around his shoulders, holding him in place. As his friends smiled, Will finally was able to swing his neck around to see who had grabbed him.

"Jackie! What's up big guy?" Will said.

Jackie Bevins had been a standout running back for the Bearcats in the fall. He had accepted a scholarship offer to play football at Valley Tech the following year. Since football season had ended, though, Will had rarely seen his friend.

"Hey, Will. Hey, guys. Is everyone here for the game tonight?" Jackie asked.

"Yeah, we are," Will said. "Man ... where have you been the last six weeks? I think I've seen you once since the season ended."

"Working out almost every day ... that's what I've been doing," Jackie said. "They hit a lot harder in college. I've got to get myself ready."

"Well, you should at least drop by sometime. Let us know you're doing OK. My mom asks about you all the time. She's getting tired of me saying, 'I haven't seen him'."

"I will ... I will," Jackie said. "Hey, I gotta run. My mom's meeting with some financial aid people today and I need to go find her."

"Brick building on the left. Third door on the right when you go in," Will said.

"You really *do* know this place, don't you?" Jackie said, smiling.

"Too well," Will said.

"Later, guys," Jackie said as he turned to leave.

The foursome made its way to the quad in the middle of campus. They sat and admired the cool weather and watched college students going about their leisure activities on a Saturday afternoon.

Soon it was time to head to the arena.

They watched as the Mustangs came from behind in the second half to post a close win. Cam re-introduced himself to Coach Pettitt, who sat with Steve and Alicia for the second half of the game.

"Maybe I'll play basketball *and* football at Valley Tech," Cam whispered to Will.

"I don't think that's done much anymore," Will said. Cam wasn't sure if his friend was talking about the landscape of college athletics or taking a good-natured shot at his athletic ability. He chose to believe It was the former.

"College is going to be pretty cool, huh?" Cam said after a brief silence.

"That's a long time from now," Will reminded him.

Chapter 15

The Bearcats had an important week ahead of them. They would face the Morris Minutemen on Tuesday before traveling to Greenfield for a conference showdown. The winner of the Greenfield game would be the frontrunner to gain the top seed in the conference tournament.

Will reminded himself that the conference championship was all he had to play for in junior high. It was a bit of a letdown, he admitted to himself, after playing in the state playoffs in football. To his friends and teammates who hadn't tasted varsity football, though, a junior high conference title was a big deal. He was going to make sure he approached it the same way.

Things remained cool between Will and Bryce in practice on Monday and again when the team ate a pregame meal together on Tuesday before hosting Morris. Their eyes met occasionally but it seemed as if each was just checking to see where the other was.

Will had sworn Shelby to secrecy about Kyle being involved in the vandalism at his house. He trusted that she wouldn't say anything. It amazed him that he'd grown so close to Shelby so quickly, even with her living an hour away. He was now sharing things with her that he hadn't told Cam, his best friend.

Cam has trouble keeping a secret, Will reminded himself. It wasn't that he didn't want to share it with Cam and it wasn't that Cam wouldn't *try* to keep quiet about it. Actually keeping the secret was tough for Cam, though, and Will didn't need anyone else knowing what he knew.

"I'm going for 20 tonight," Cam said to any teammate within earshot. Even Coach Hammett heard the comment, which he dismissed quickly with a roll of his eyes. "Coach, did I tell you I'm going to Valley Tech to play?"

"Oh really?" Coach Hammett said sarcastically. "When is this going to happen?"

"Three more years, Coach, and I'll be there," Cam said. "They pretty much put the offer on the table on Saturday."

Ty, seated between Will and Cam, snickered.

"Three more years, huh?" Coach Hammett said. "Tell you what, Cam. That sounds like a great goal. Let's try to take care of tonight's game first. Would that be OK?"

"Sure, Coach," Cam grinned.

Baltic came out on fire in the first half against Morris. The Minutemen had lost just once in conference play and the Bearcats had expected more of a challenge. They didn't get it that night, though. Cam, true to his word, scored his 20 points – all in the first half, and the Bearcats rolled to an easy victory. Will had come off the bench again and scored 12 points, all on three-point shots.

"OK, guys," Coach Hammett told the team afterward. "You've put yourselves in a great position. If you don't take advantage of it, though, all those games we've won won't really mean anything. We have a little trip to Greenfield coming up on Friday. Win that one and we're in the driver's seat."

The Bearcats needed no extra motivation in facing the Greenfield Goblins. Aside from neighboring Bridgeport, the Greenfield game was typically the biggest of the year for Baltic teams in any sport. The players knew from the time they were old enough to attend a game that it was important to beat those two teams. The Greenfield game had become even bigger in recent years since the Goblins dropped into Baltic's classification. As conference rivals, it seemed a title was usually on the line when the teams got together.

"The varsity boys will be playing right after you guys Friday and it's a big game for us, too," Coach Hammett continued. "I expect you all to hang around and support them, if you can."

That would be no problem for Will. One of the best things about playing in the same conference as Greenfield was that he was given more opportunities to see Shelby. That he'd get to watch a good basketball game at the same time was just a bonus.

Steve Stover was on his telephone when Alicia, Will and Ty arrived home after the game.

"OK. No, no, that's fine," he was saying. "I was just wondering if any progress had been made. No, if he's not in, I'll just check with him later. OK. Thanks."

He turned and gave the boys each a quick hug.

"Great game tonight, both of you," he said. Turning to his wife, he shook his head. "Still nothing from the police about who did all this. Did you file the insurance claim?"

"Yes, did it right after it happened," Alicia said.

"It's hard to believe two people walked – or drove, right into this neighborhood and managed to do that much damage and no one saw anything," Steve said. "It's not even about the money. I'd just like to know if there's someone out there who dislikes us this much."

Will tried to ignore the one-sided conversation. He could feel his dad's eyes on him, though.

"Will, do you really think he would do this?"

Will knew immediately he was talking about Bryce.

"Like you said earlier, Dad," Will said, "we have no idea who did this."

The sarcasm was evident. Will knew his father was well aware of his rough history with Bryce.

"I'd just like to know if that kid did this or not, that's all," he said. "Who does he hang around with? Who are his closest friends?"

Will's teeth sank into his tongue. He knew his father likely had no idea about the dating scene at Baltic High School and wouldn't have cared if he had known. Will wasn't about to even whisper Kyle's name at this point. There was no way his dad knew Kyle was dating Bryce's sister.

"It's kind of weird," Will said. "It doesn't seem like he really has any close friends. He just kind of mixes in with crowds of people. I don't think I've ever really seen him with one person."

Ty nodded in agreement.

"He always seems angry," Ty said. "I don't think that means he broke our backboards and threw eggs at our house and scared our sister half to death, though."

"Well, we're going to find out sooner or later," Steve said. "One thing kids can't do for very long is stay quiet when they do something like this."

Chapter 16

Wednesday and Thursday passed at a snail's pace as Will waited for another chance to spend time with Shelby.

He didn't tell her – didn't mention to anyone – that he was beginning to notice Missy Starling more and more. He hadn't really known Missy until she asked him to be her escort in the Homecoming assembly in the fall. He'd obliged and it brought him and Shelby close to their first argument.

Now, with Shelby gone, his eyes would occasionally wander. He and Missy had two classes together, so it was a little tough to *not* notice her. It also didn't help – or hurt, for that matter - that she was now the prettiest girl in the ninth grade.

Shelby.

Will was constantly reminding himself that Shelby was sitting in class at Greenfield thinking about him and the attention he paid to Missy would only hurt Shelby.

Of course that's what Shelby is doing, he told himself.

Friday finally arrived and Will packed his basketball gear and waited for Cam and his older brother Jake to pick him up for school. Ty and Chelsea had left earlier and his parents were out the door before anyone.

Will walked to the back door and glanced outside. He stared for a long minute at the hundreds, thousands even, dollars of sports equipment his parents had set up there. It seemed it had been there his entire life and it probably had been. Maybe even all of Chelsea's life. Will knew his dad treated Chelsea like a princess and wouldn't have traded her for another son in a million years. He also knew, though, that as soon as his sons arrived in the world, the backyard transformation had really begun.

Steve Stover had made his mark on the athletic fields and parlayed his name into several successful businesses. He was going to at least give his sons the same opportunity. To Will, his dad's reaction to the vandalism was beginning to make a little more sense. It wasn't just sports equipment to him. This was how he bonded with his sons.

The car horn snapped Will out of his daydream. He locked the front door and jogged to Jake's car.

"Big game for you boys tonight," Jake said. "I'm guessing you're both ready to play?"

"You bet!" Cam answered quickly. "Biggest game of my life. So far, anyway."

"Ready to go," Will said.

"You think the Valley Tech coach will be there tonight?" Cam asked Will. "They're not playing tonight. I checked their schedule. I'd bet he'll be there!"

"Maybe so. I really don't know, Cam," Will said. "Greenfield is tough. We'd probably be better off to spend our time thinking about the game."

Friday was a test day at Baltic High. After a first semester that was more academically challenging than any he'd ever faced, Will was back in the groove and moving through his classes with relative ease.

He finished all his exams during the first half of class. To keep down on the noise, students were instructed to report to study hall each period after turning in a test. Those who were prepared for the tests typically spent at least a half hour each period sitting and visiting in study hall under the watchful eye of Coach Peterson.

That also meant Will spent a total of three hours on Friday chatting with Missy Starling. She seemed to get more attractive each hour, Will noticed after their third meeting. Shelby had once warned him – maybe it was during the near-argument – that Missy was known for stealing other girls' boyfriends. Perhaps tempting fate, Will continued to find himself seated close to Missy each time he arrived in study hall. They chatted quietly about the exam they'd just taken, the one coming up, the basketball game that night.

Missy never asked about Shelby.

Feeling guiltier than ever, Will decided enough was enough. It was more than coincidence that the only seat open each time he entered just happened to be the one next to Missy. During his last exam of the day, Will doubled his focus, hoping it would take him longer to complete. He still finished early, though, and went directly to Coach Peterson's desk when he entered the study hall.

"Hey Coach," he said. He'd barely seen Coach Peterson since football had ended. "I have a few questions about something we did on offense this year. Can I sit up here the rest of the class?"

"Sure," Coach said. "Shouldn't you be focused on basketball, though? That's a big game coming up tonight."

"Oh, sure. I am," Will said. "There were just a couple of things my dad was asking about with our offense. It bothered me that I couldn't explain some of it."

The tactic worked. Coach Peterson was always ready to talk football and Will was able to hide from Missy, at least for a little while.

With the top seed in the conference tournament on the line, the Baltic starting five picked the worst possible moment to play its worst basketball of the season. Not only that, but the win streak had reached 14 games and no Bearcat wanted to see it end there.

Ty was uncharacteristically sloppy with the basketball. Greenfield's pressure defense forced him into several first-quarter turnovers and the Goblins took a quick 10-2 lead before Coach Hammett could signal for a timeout.

Will had his shooting jacket off and was ready to check in when Coach Hammett called him back from the scorer's table. Now down 14-2, Will wondered if Coach had changed his mind about putting him in the game.

"Instead of replacing Luke, send Bryce out," Coach Hammett said, pointing Will back to the scorer's table. In a matter of seconds, a foul was called. As the teams lined up for the free throw attempt, the horn sounded and Will trotted onto the floor. Luke instinctively lowered his head and started for the bench.

"No, not you Luke," Will called quickly. "Bryce, you're out."

"What!" Will thought he heard Bryce yell but quickly realized it wasn't Bryce. The shout had come from behind the Bearcats' bench. Will and the rest of the Baltic players looked into the stands and saw Officer Locklin on the third row, standing and red-faced.

When the heads turned toward him, Officer Locklin quickly regained his composure and sat. Bryce walked slowly off the court. It was tough for Will to tell if he was angry, embarrassed or both.

Without Bryce's presence around the basket, the Bearcats compensated with more outside shooting. Luke, seizing an unexpected chance to stay on the court, nailed back-to-back three-pointers before Ty fed Cam for a layup and then Will for another three-pointer. Less than two minutes after Will had checked in, Cam stepped outside for a long-range jump shot of his own that put Baltic ahead for the first time.

Bryce played sparingly in the second half as the Bearcats kept up the hot shooting from the outside. Will finished with 17 points and Luke had 16 as Baltic won easily.

Chapter 17

Coach Hammett excused himself quickly from the locker room. His bigger chore of the night was still to come as the varsity teams from each school were already on the floor warming up. Bryce also dressed quickly and left the gym. Someone said later that Officer Locklin left sometime during the fourth quarter, still seething.

Will, Ty and Cam greeted their parents in the stands before Will left in search of Shelby. He hadn't seen her during the game. At least he knew she hadn't sat with his parents. They hadn't seen her, either. Will sent Shelby a text message: "Are you here?"

It took Shelby less than a minute to respond.

"Sorry. I was there for a little while but I had to get home to study for a big test tomorrow," she wrote. "Maybe we can get together this weekend."

Somewhat stunned, Will stared at his phone. Shelby had known for at least a month that he'd be in Greenfield that night, for that game. In all likelihood, she'd known about the test that long also. Shrugging to himself, he climbed the stairs and sat back down with his family and friends.

"Is she here?" Will's mother asked.

"No, studying," Will answered quietly. Alicia could tell he was hurt.

"Well, studying comes first," Alicia said with more compassion than was really needed.

"Hey, great game!" The words came from behind Will and, before he could turn, he recognized Missy's voice and felt his body tense as she hugged him from behind.

"Ah, thanks," Will said. He glanced around quickly to see who all was taking in the scene. His dad and Ty were focused on the game. Cam rolled his eyes and slowly gave Will a disapproving look. Alicia wasn't missing anything.

"Hi, Mrs. Stover! Didn't Will play a great game? I don't think they would have won if it hadn't been for him. He really played great, don't you think?" Missy's words were coming faster than most people could listen.

"Hi Missy," Alicia said. "Yes, the whole team played great. You cheerleaders did a great job, too." She turned her attention back to the game before Missy could respond.

"Anyone sitting here?" Missy asked Will. Before he could answer, she swung her leg over the row in front of her and hopped into the seat next to Will.

"So ... where's your girlfriend?"

"She's studying," Will mumbled.

"Didn't she know you were playing here tonight?" Missy asked loud enough for the entire section to hear. "You guys didn't break up, did you?" She gave Will her best sarcastic sad face.

"No. We didn't break up," Will said. "She has a big test tomorrow."

"Oh, that's good. You two are so cute together," Missy said. "Of course, I have a picture on my nightstand from the Homecoming assembly that's pretty cute, too."

Will was beginning to wonder how to escape when Missy continued.

"Exactly why are you guys still dating?"

"Excuse me?" Will was beginning to get annoyed. Yes, he reminded himself, it was possible to get annoyed with Missy, no matter how pretty she was.

"I mean … isn't it inconvenient? You guys live an hour apart. How long do you think that's going to last?"

"We're making it work," Will said. "It hasn't really been a big deal … yet."

"So … you think it *will* turn into a big deal?"

"No. That's not what I meant," Will said. "Everything is fine with us. We still see each other pretty often."

"Except for tonight," Missy said, leaning closer to Will. "When you have a basketball game … in the town where she lives?"

"It's the exception, not the rule," Will said smiling at her. "Really, it's not a big deal."

"Whatever you say," Missy said.

Like most 14-year-olds, Will realized that Missy sitting next to him in a huge arena would soon have the entire junior high talking. He caught several looks from teammates. Luckily, he told himself, Bryce was gone and that would keep him from being the one to alert Shelby.

The Baltic varsity was having a tough time with the bigger, stronger Greenfield team and trailed at the half, 33-21. Coach Hammett didn't look pleased as the teams left the floor.

"Maybe we should go play for them," Cam, seated on the other wide of Will, said. "Seriously, I think we could play them closer than … "

"Uh oh," Cam said quietly, elbowing Will in the ribs. He nodded toward the entrance to the arena, across the floor from where they were seated. There stood Shelby, staring toward their seats.

She wasn't smiling.

Before Missy could realize what had happened, Will quickly popped out of his seat and took off. He yelled back over his shoulder, "Be back in a bit. Gotta talk to someone."

He took the stairs down to the floor level two at a time and nearly sprinted for the exit, hoping to beat Shelby to the door. He barely made it, intercepting her by the arm as she headed outside. Shelby tugged her arm away, refusing to look at Will.

"Hey, you made it," Will said.

"Big gym," Shelby said, turning to face Will. A tear had already found its way halfway down her cheek. "Apparently, it's not big enough."

"What?" Will asked, doing his best to play off what he knew was coming.

"What's wrong?"

"Her," Shelby said, moving away from the door and to a corner where they wouldn't be overheard. "That's what's wrong. I begged my mom for a half hour, asking to come back up here so I could see you. I think I'd better go, Will."

"No, please don't," Will pleaded. "Nothing is going on, OK? I was sitting there and she came and sat by me. It's not like we're on a date or something."

"I'm sure that's what she's planning, though," Shelby said, brushing away the tear. Anger was moving in to take its place.

"Don't make this bigger than it is," Will said. "She's a friend. We have classes together. It's nothing. She knows all about you and about us."

"Do you remember what I told you about her at Homecoming?" Shelby asked quietly. "Do you?"

"Yeah, I remember," Will said. "And I won't let that happen."

They stared at each other for a full minute, neither speaking. Finally, Will broke the silence.

"Can we go sit down?"

"Not up there," Shelby said.

"OK, on the other side. As long as I'm sitting with you, I don't care where it is," Will said.

Chapter 18

The conference tournament included all eight teams in the league, seeded by how they finished in the regular season. Baltic, with its unbeaten record, was the top seed. Once-beaten Greenfield was seeded second.

"Looks like another game with Greenfield," Cam said when Will showed him a copy of the bracket. "And, that will be our last game. This undefeated season has seemed rather easy."

"Slow down there, big boy," Will said. "Let's take it one game at a time. Besides the Greenfield game, we really haven't played that well lately. We could be in for a rough week. Let's just make sure we don't get ahead of ourselves. We can celebrate when it's all over. Until then, let's stay focused."

"Yes sir, Coach," Cam said mockingly. "Where is the tournament, anyway?"

"Morris," Will said. "And their fans are nuts. It should be interesting. Remember, they played us really tough before."

"Their fans *are* a bit crazy," Cam said. "It sure makes it fun to play there, though. We won't have to play Morris again. They're on Greenfield's side of the bracket. Didn't you notice? And Greenfield has already beaten them once."

"Might not be as easy this time," Will said.

The Baltic juniors had been matched up with Johnson Prep, which staggered into the game with a 1-15 overall record. It had not won a single game in the conference season. During Monday's practice, Coach Hammett echoed Will's earlier comments.

"Now is not the time to take any team for granted," he told the team. "We have three games left this season, if we do what we need to do to advance. Here's another way to look at it, guys. The next time we lose, we're finished. That means we're in the same position as everyone else. It's real simple from here. Win and you move on. Lose and you're finished."

The Bearcats seemed to take the advice to heart. They gave an inspired effort in practice. As it was winding down, the team broke into several groups to work on free throws. Will, Ty, Cam and Luke eased away to a side goal and began to go through their five-shot rotations. Soon after they began, Bryce walked over and stood next to Will.

"You guys have room for one more?" he asked.

"Sure. We have the smallest group," Will said. It was the longest voluntary conversation the two had engaged in since Will confronted him about the vandalism.

Little else was said, though, as the shooting continued.

Even with Will playing one of the biggest roles on the team, Coach Hammett had continued to use him as the first substitute off the bench. Will had not been happy with the role. He'd never been on a team – in any sport – as a benchwarmer. He saw the bigger picture, though, and did his best when he was called upon. He usually wound up playing as much, or more, than any of the starters besides Cam. Coach Hammett liked chemistry, though, and had decided it would be foolish to starting moving parts around.

They both realized, especially after their talk early in the season, that the perfect season was within their grasp. That, after all, was the most important goal.

If the Bearcats had wanted to take any game for granted, the game with Johnson Prep would have been a good choice. Baltic was simply too much for the Wildcats and mostly Bearcat seventh graders played the majority of the second half. Ian, who had been a starter until Ty took the spot from him, dribbled out most of the fourth quarter in an effort to keep the game from getting even more out of hand.

Cam scored 26 points, all in the first eight minutes of the game, then had watched the remainder from the bench. Baltic won easily, 70-19.

"That wasn't very exciting," Cam said to Will as the last minutes ticked off the clock. "I think our seventh graders could have played the whole game and beaten them."

"Just two more," Will said, grinning. After pocketing a state championship – and the ring that came with it – in the football season, he was happy to be within reach of another title. Especially one he could enjoy with his best friend.

Vero was up next for the Bearcats. A bit more of a challenge, perhaps, but the Baltic juniors were still having a tough time staying focused on the task at hand and not thinking ahead to a rematch with Greenfield.

The Bearcats hadn't faced Vero during the regular season because of a flu outbreak in the Vero schools. In fact, the Hawks had missed nearly half the conference schedule because of the epidemic.

"They're a bit of an unknown," Will told Cam. "I don't know anyone who has seen them play this year. They only lost once, but the coaches didn't seed them very high because they missed so many games."

The Hawks looked like they were making up for lost time when the teams took the floor at Morris High School on Thursday. Consistently outrunning the Bearcats down the floor, Vero converted several easy layups and took an early 12-4 advantage.

Will entered the lineup replacing Bryce, who was huffing after chasing the Hawks around for the first four minutes of the game. He almost looked relieved to take a place on the bench. Will wasted little time making his presence felt. Sitting and watching the first minutes of the game, he had noticed a Vero player breaking to the sideline each time a shot went into the air. Will knew that's where the Hawks' fast break was starting and if he could stop the initial pass, the entire break might fall apart.

Ty took an off-balance shot in the lane and, as soon as Will saw the ball in the air, he sprinted to where he knew the outlet pass would go. He guessed correctly, intercepted the pass and pulled up for a 12-foot shot off the glass.

Good.

Catching on, Ty picked off the next pass and moved to the offensive end. He found Cam inside, who immediately whipped a bullet of a pass out to Will in the corner for a three-pointer.

Good.

After a Vero timeout, the game settled into slowdown mode, which the Baltic juniors preferred. Bryce re-entered, replacing Luke, and played like a madman. He pulled down nearly every offensive rebound there was. Some he put right back in for easy baskets, others he found open shooters who were launching three-pointers as fast as the scoreboard operator could move the digits.

Baltic scored the last 12 points of the game, making the final score of 58-34 look a lot more impressive than it actually was.

The mood in the jubilant locker room was quickly tempered by Coach Hammett, who settled his team into a tight circle before speaking in a hushed tone.

"Guys, great job tonight," he said. "I'm glad you're happy with the way you played because you deserve to be."

He stopped for a second and waited for the words to come.

"When we started this season, way back in December, I wouldn't have believed we'd be in the position we're in. We've got a chance to do something that's never been done at Baltic. Every year the goals I have for my team are the same: Win the conference regular season and then win the conference tournament. We're close to accomplishing that. What we rarely talk about, though, is going through an entire season undefeated. You guys have been challenged a couple of times this year and you're probably going to be challenged again. Let's stay focused on getting one more win, guys."

Chapter 19

Ty opened the door and smiled at Mrs. Caldwell, the family's next-door neighbor for the past 14 years.

"Hello, Ty," Mrs. Caldwell said. Glancing over his shoulder, she said softly, "Are your parents home?"

"Yes, ma'am, just a second," he said. "Come on in."

Alicia Stover made her way through the foyer and into the living room. She gave Mrs. Caldwell a fast hug hello and joined her on the sofa.

"Hi Alicia," she said. "I don't want to be a bother but I wanted to talk with you and Steve about something. Is he home also?"

"Yes. Is everything alright?" Alicia asked as she motioned to the kitchen for her husband to join them.

"Yes, yes."

"Hi, Mary Sue. How are you?" Steve greeted his neighbor.

"Oh, I'm fine," she said. She glanced nervously at Chelsea and Ty, who were watching a television program in the room. Barely above a whisper, she said, "Steve, Alicia … would it be OK to talk in private for a minute?"

"Certainly. Are you sure everything is alright?" Steve repeated as he signaled for the children to leave.

"Yes. I saw something you might be interested in," she said. "A few weeks ago."

She interrupted herself.

"This might all be settled now. If it is, I sincerely apologize. I don't mean to be nosy but something I saw has been bothering me and I thought I should talk with you two about it."

"Sure. What did you see?" Alicia asked.

"Well, it was the night everything happened over here," she began, just loud enough for them to hear. "I heard something that night and looked out the bedroom window. I got a pretty good look at the two who messed up everything over here."

"Did you recognize either of them?" Steve asked.

"I didn't at the time, but like I said, I got a really good look at both of them. One was a boy, probably Will's age."

"How about the other one?" Alicia asked.

"It was a man," Mary Sue said. "I had never seen him before but I've seen him since then."

"Where have you seen him?" Steve asked.

"In your back yard."

"Huh?" The conversation was getting more confusing by the second for Steve.

"The police officer," Mary Sue said. "You and the boys were talking to him the day after this happened. You were talking in the back yard. I was feeding the dog and saw him then."

"You're saying the police officer – Mr. Locklin – is the man you saw the night before. You're saying he helped do all this?" Steve and Alicia were too stunned to immediately be angry.

"I'm positive that's who it was," she said. "I even recognized his voice. He never said the boy's name but he was telling him what to do, like it was his plan or something."

"Oh my," Alicia said. "It was night, Mary Sue. How can you be certain he's the man you saw?"

"I'm positive," Mrs. Caldwell said. "I'd bet my life on it. They couldn't see me because of the shade but I could see them perfectly."

"Hold on a second," Steve said, hurriedly leaving the room. He returned a minute later with a Baltic Junior High yearbook. He flipped several pages, then gently placed it in Mary Sue's lap.

"Do you recognize anyone on this page?" he asked.

"Besides Will, you mean?"

They laughed.

"Yes, besides Will. Anyone else there that you've seen before?"

She studied the book, up a row, down the next. Then, she paused.

"This one right here. He was here. That's the boy I saw," she said. Her index finger rested on the smiling face of Bryce Locklin.

"You're positive?" Steve asked again, hoping for just a bit of uncertainty.

"Positive, Steve," she said.

"Oh, great," he said.

"I'm guessing you know him?" Mary Sue asked.

"Unfortunately," Steve said, then looked at Alicia. "Do you know where the Locklins moved here from?"

"Yes, they came from Miriam, down just across the state line," she said. "Why?"

"Lots of old teammates, that's why," Steve answered. "I figured I'd have an old teammate in about any place you might name. Harold Green lives in Miriam … has for years. I think I need to give him a call."

Mary Sue apologized again for being "nosy" and said goodbye.

Steve was listening to Harold Green's phone ring before Alicia had the front door closed.

"Hey, Hal, it's Steve Stover. How are you?"

"Good. Good here, too. Everyone's fine. You have just a minute to chat?"

Alicia rejoined Steve, who warned Harold that he was putting the phone on speaker. From the kitchen, Will had overheard much of Mary Sue's news and was now listening in.

"Alicia, how are you? It's been a long time. You guys don't get down here enough," Harold said.

"We're good. Unfortunately, there's not a real good reason for the call," Steve said.

"What's up, buddy?"

"Are you familiar with a guy named Locklin from down there?" Steve asked.

"Buddy Locklin?" Harold said quickly, with a chuckle. "Has a son named Bryce and an older daughter, Maggie?"

"Yeah, that's him," Steve said. "What can you tell me about him?"

"Don't tell me … there's a problem, right?"

"How'd you know?" Steve asked.

"Problems seem to follow these folks. Well, Buddy, anyway," Harold said. "They moved from here a few years back but I didn't know where they'd landed. What do you need to know about him?"

"How long has he been a police officer?" Steve asked.

"A WHAT!"

"He's a police officer," Steve repeated. "You didn't know that?"

"Please tell me you're joking," Harold said.

"Nope," Steve said. "I wish I was."

"And ... he carries a gun?"

"He does," Steve said. "Is that a bad thing?"

"I'm just wondering how he passed a background check," Harold said. "Listen Steve. I've known the guy longer than I've known you. Grew up here with him. He's always had some anger issues. What'd he do, anyway?"

"Well ... we think he and Bryce vandalized our house," Steve said, foregoing most of the details.

"Sounds about right," Harold said. "A police officer. Wow. He was really big in youth sports when they lived here. The big joke was that the guy had never seen the end of a game because he'd always been kicked out before it was over. I saw him get kicked out of games that Bryce wasn't even playing."

"He seems to have gotten things under control a bit, then," Steve said. "Besides vandalizing my house, I mean. Bryce and Will have played together for a couple of years now and I hadn't even really met the guy until this happened."

"Besides vandalizing my house," Harold repeated Steve's words. "You're still a pretty funny guy, Steve."

"Thanks, Hal," Steve said. "Hey, I appreciate the information. I'll let you know how things turn out. Let me know if you're ever in Greenfield for a game or passing through Baltic. We'll get together."

"Sounds good, Steve. Bye."

Will walked into the room as his dad clicked off the phone.

"Oh boy. This isn't good," he said.

"You hear everything?" his dad asked.

"Yes sir. I think so," Will said. "This is really not good."

"No, son, it's not," Steve said.

Will agonized most of the night over what to do. He'd stayed up late discussing things with his parents, who had insisted it wasn't something he needed to involve himself with.

"This happened because of me, though," Will had told Steve and Alicia. "I just didn't expect adults to have been in the middle of something like this."

"People will surprise you sometimes," Steve told him. "The older you get, the more you'll see it."

From what Will could tell, his dad planned to visit the Baltic Police Department the next day. Will didn't know what that might mean for Officer Locklin or Bryce. He suddenly felt he understood Bryce a little better though. Some of the things he'd done and the attitude he displayed made more sense now.

He'd almost forgotten that he'd practically accused Kyle of being involved. He'd even told Shelby as much. Besides dating Bryce's sister, it didn't seem that Kyle could be more innocent. Before the sun came up, Will had decided he needed to talk with Kyle.

He found him in the hallway before school. Luckily, neither Bryce nor Maggie were anywhere around at the time.

"Hey Kyle, can I talk to you for a minute? Somewhere in private?"

"Sure. What's up?" Kyle asked.

"I think I owe you an apology," Will began.

"For what?"

"Well ... I've kind of been assuming that you were with Bryce when he vandalized my house. Two different people have told us there were two people there. We were pretty certain Bryce was one of them and I thought maybe the other was you."

"Well, it wasn't," Kyle interrupted. He seemed to want to finish the awkward conversation.

"I know ... I know that now," Will said. "We know who the other guy was."

"You do?"

"Yes," Will said.

"You're positive?" Kyle asked.

"Yep."

"Well ... who was it?"

"Their dad."

A long pause followed. It seemed the only surprise on Kyle's face was that Will now knew.

"Is your dad going to press charges?" Kyle finally asked.

"I don't know what he's going to do," Will said. "It's something you kind of have to deal with, though ... ya know?"

"I guess you do," Kyle admitted. "Listen, I'll find you at lunch. We need to talk more."

"OK," Will said.

Will made a quick trip to the office and asked to use the school telephone. He phoned his father and stepped into an empty room to keep from being overheard.

"Dad, can you wait until after school before you go to the police department?" he asked. "I think there might be more to this. Please wait until we talk before you do anything."

"No problem, son," Steve said. "Everything OK?"

"I think so. Just please don't go until we have a chance to talk," Will said.

"OK."

Kyle was waiting for Will when the bell rang that sent the students to lunch. Kyle wasted little time and began to speak as they walked toward the gymnasium.

"There's a lot more to this, Will," Kyle said. "Mr. Locklin has a few anger management issues. I guess that's a nice way to say it. Maggie thinks he's getting help for it. She doesn't know about him being in the middle of this. I think she probably guessed that Bryce might be involved but she doesn't know her dad was there."

"Oh," Will said.

"Yeah. This is going to crush her," Kyle said. "She really loves her dad. She told me about some of the things he did when she was younger ... before they moved here. Said she was always embarrassed at how he acted. But, he's her dad and she loves him."

Will kept listening.

"I only know about this because Bryce told me what happened. He said it was his dad's idea and I believe him. Bryce is a good kid, Will. But he's going to do whatever his dad tells him to do, no matter how outlandish it might be. He only told me because he wants help for his dad. He's embarrassed, Will."

"What does Officer Locklin have against me?" Will asked.

"You're everything he wants Bryce to be," Kyle said. "Great student. Great athlete. Nice guy." Everyone likes you. Believe me, your name is mentioned a lot around that house."

"That's a little creepy," Will said.

"Yeah, it is," Kyle admitted. "Will, I'm not sure what you guys are going to do or how you want to handle this. I just want you to understand why Bryce is the way he is."

"Thanks, Kyle," Will said. "I'm not sure what'll happen, either. It's kind of up to my parents. I asked my dad not to do anything until we talked and he agreed."

"Good. Thanks, Will."

Bryce, possibly tipped off by Kyle that Will knew about his dad's involvement, didn't show up for practice on Wednesday. It was the day before the final game - and the biggest game - of the season. He had been in Geometry class with Will earlier in the day.

Will was summoned to Coach Hammett's office as soon as he entered the gym.

"Bryce quit the team," Coach Hammett said.

"He did what?"

"Yep. With the biggest game of the year coming up, he came by and told me he wouldn't be playing anymore," Coach said. "At least he came by to tell me."

Will dropped his head.

"Coach, there are some things going on with Bryce right now. Things that he has very little control over. Can I make a suggestion?"

"Sure. What is it?" Coach Hammett asked.

"Let's just get through practice today. Can we just say he won't be in practice today? Call it a personal issue or something. Let me talk to him first ... before he's officially off the team?" Will asked.

"You do realize you're keeping yourself from being in the starting lineup tomorrow night? Isn't that what you've wanted all year? And, I know you and Bryce have never gotten along. Will, he just walked out on this team with our biggest game coming up."

"Trust me, Coach. Just let me talk to him first," Will said. "Let's just say he really needs this team ... really needs something good to happen right now."

"Talk to him and keep me in the loop," Coach Hammett said. "And, you don't breathe a word of this to anyone."

"No problem, Coach," Will said. "And thanks."

Chapter 20

Immediately after practice, Will had Chelsea drop him off at their father's office.

"Hey Dad," he said as he entered. "We need to talk."

"Yes we do," Steve said, motioning to the seat across from his. "Bryce came by here this afternoon."

"Seriously?" Will said.

"Yep. Told me everything ... without my asking," Steve said. "He told me his dad was there ... that it was his dad's idea ... that Officer Locklin has always had a problem with you, with us, I guess."

"Wow," was all Will could manage.

"Yeah, some strange stuff," Steve said. "I'll say this, though. It took some guts for a 14-year-old kid to come in here and admit all that to me."

"I guess it did," Will said. "I actually need to go find him and talk to him. He quit the team today."

"You're kidding," Steve said. "With one game left?"

"Yes sir," Will said. "I don't think he wanted to, though. I think he just did it so he wouldn't have to face me."

"Well, let's go see if we can fix this," Mr. Stover said, pulling on his coat.

Steve and Will arrived at Bryce's house just as Officer Locklin was coming home. He gave them a worried glance and pulled his police car into the driveway.

Stepping out of the car, he smiled and asked, "Hello gentlemen. What can I do for the Stovers today?"

"Wait here," Steve said to Will and opened the door.

"Hello Buddy," Steve said. "You have a few minutes to talk?"

"Sure ... sure," he said, faking a smile. "Everything alright? Let's go to the back. We can talk on the deck."

"Well, not really," Steve said, glancing back at Will. "We've talked to a couple of people who saw the vandals."

"Oh, really?" Officer Locklin said, stopping in his tracks.

"Yeah. Buddy, I'm not one to waste a lot of time talking in circles," Steve said. "Someone saw you there with Bryce. They're 100 percent positive it was you and they're willing to go to the police - your employer - and tell them."

"Is that so?" Officer Locklin said. "I'd prefer you call me 'Officer', if it's all the same."

"If that's what you want," Steve said. "Listen. I'm willing to talk this out and settle it the best way possible. I don't want to be responsible for someone losing his job and everything that might come from that."

There was a long pause before Mr. Stover spoke again.

"I know there have been some problems in the past," he said. "Hal Green and I played together at Valley Tech. I spoke with him about you. He filled me in."

Another long pause.

"I'll make you a deal, Officer," Steve said. "If you'll go to counseling and get some help with this, I'll agree to forget the whole thing."

Officer Locklin dropped his head, shaking it slowly.

"Buddy, listen," Steve said. "You've got a wonderful family. Bryce is a good kid. He and Maggie really look up to you and they love you. But they want you to get some help for this. Do we have a deal?"

Fortunately, Officer Locklin knew when to accept a deal.

"Yes, we have a deal," he said quietly. "I'm really sorry, Steve. Do you have estimates on what I owe you?"

"You don't owe me anything," Steve said. "That's all been taken care of. You owe it to your family to change. I know a couple of people who might be able to help. I'd be glad to recommend them."

Officer Locklin looked stunned.

"I'll pay you back ... every penny of it," he said.

"You get the help we're talking about and I'll feel you've paid me back," Steve said. "We do have one small problem that needs to be fixed, though."

"What's that?"

"Well, Bryce decided to quit the team today. I think it's because he thought this was all going to come out and he was embarrassed about it," Steve said. "This team is on the verge of accomplishing something kids only dream of being a part of. They need him on the floor. And, I think he needs this team."

"OK. I'll talk to him and see what I can do," Officer Locklin said as the two headed back to the driveway. As they rounded the corner of the house, they saw Bryce leaning into the Stover's car, saying something to Will. Not sure of what was going on, they upped their pace to the car.

"Hey guys," Steve said. "Everything OK here?"

"Yes sir," Bryce said, stepping back. "I just called Coach Hammett. I think we have everything worked out."

"OK. That's great," Steve said, glancing at Will. Will nodded to confirm Bryce's words.

"Alicia's waiting for us," Steve said. "We've got to get home." He turned and shook Buddy's hand, then put a hand on Bryce's shoulder.

"Biggest game of your life tomorrow night, son," he said. "Not many guys can say they were unbeaten in football and basketball in the same year."

"Yes sir," Bryce said, smiling. "That would be pretty cool."

"Later, guys," Steve said as they drove away.

Will, Cam and Ty boarded the bus together and found seats. It had seemed the school day lasted a week. The boys had tried to focus on the schoolwork but thoughts of their final basketball game kept creeping in. Bryce was one of the last to board the bus. Seeing him alone, Will caught his eye and stuck up a hand, motioning Bryce to join him.

Ty, because he lived in the same house as Will, was aware of the happenings in the Locklin family. Cam knew the major points but had been spared the details. He knew nothing about Bryce's dad being involved and the Stovers aimed to keep it that way.

"You ready for this?" Will asked when Bryce was seated.

"I am," he answered. "I hadn't really thought about what your dad said yesterday. Undefeated in football and basketball. That's something we'll remember for a while."

"I'd think that's something you remember forever," Will said. "Of course, we have to go actually do it, first."

"Right," Bryce said with a grin.

Coach Hammett echoed the importance of what his team was trying to accomplish when they gathered in the locker room.

"Guys, this is it," he said. "This is why you play the game. You've put yourselves in a position to do something that most people never do. I never played on an undefeated team. Ever. You guys have that chance."

He continued.

"Trust me, guys. It's rare and it's something you'll always have. This will create a bond between you that'll probably never be broken. Now, relax, play hard and enjoy yourselves."

It wasn't Greenfield, as had been expected, waiting for the Bearcats, though. Morris, playing in its own gym, had surprised the Goblins in the semifinals and was now waiting for a chance to spoil Baltic's perfect season. The hometown crowd had filled the gym, something not usually seen in a junior high game.

Much like the first meeting between the two teams, the Minutemen started fast. A three-pointer late in the quarter gave Morris a 15-6 lead at the first break.

"OK, guys," Coach Hammett told his team as they huddled. "The nerves should be gone now. Remember what got you here and let's see some of that this quarter. Will, you're in for Luke."

The talk rejuvenated the Bearcats, who immediately went on a 12-0 run to take a small lead. The teams traded baskets the rest of the half and Baltic led 26-23 at the intermission.

Despite a great effort, the Bearcats couldn't pull away in the third quarter. Each time they made a run, the Morris supporters would rally their team. Physically, Baltic was the better team but the Minutemen weren't willing to give in. Will's three-point shot at the third quarter buzzer kept the Bearcats in front, 42-39.

"One quarter, guys," Coach Hammett implored as they gathered for one of the last times. "Keep your heads out there and play solid defense. Be patient on offense and work for a great shot. Not a good one ... a great one."

Morris made a final push in the fourth quarter, hoping it would be enough.

The Minutemen took advantage of Cam picking up his fourth foul and went inside every trip down the floor. Unable to successfully defend for fear of fouling out, Cam was helpless against the Morris post players. At the same time, Will suddenly went cold from the floor, missing on three consecutive three-point shots.

Morris led 51-46 with 1:21 left in the game when Coach Hammett signaled for his final timeout.

"Bryce, Cam needs help in there. You've got to come over and help out when his man gets the ball inside," Coach said. "Ty ... Will ... someone needs to make a play offensively."

The buzzer sounded, sending the teams back to the court.

Morris immediately went back inside against Cam. As soon as his man caught the pass, though, Bryce streaked across and knocked the ball away from behind. Ty took it in the air and sped down the court for a layup, cutting the lead to 51-48 with 58 seconds left. Morris held the ball for 30 seconds on the next possession, finally getting it back inside. Cam was called for his fifth foul and was forced from the game. The Minutemen fans exploded in cheers as he left the floor.

"Great job, son," Coach Hammett told him as Cam took a seat and wiped his face with a towel.

With 24 seconds left, the Morris player missed both free throws. Bryce grabbed the rebound and shoveled the ball to Ty, who raced up the court. It appeared Ty was taking the ball all the way to the goal but he stopped as the Morris defense regrouped and cut off the drive. Without looking, Ty sent a left-handed pass across court to the corner. He knew it was Will's favorite shooting spot on the court. Will caught the pass and, nearly in the same motion, launched a three-pointer.

The game was tied with nine seconds left. Morris called timeout to set up a last shot.

Driving to the goal and hoping for a foul, the Minutemen point guard floated a shot toward the rim as the final buzzer sounded.

The ball looked like it was going to be on target. In that brief moment, Will saw his season pass in a few snapshots: The practice skirmish with Bryce, the vandalism at his house, the argument with Shelby, Cam's insistence that he'd someday play both basketball and football in college, the past couple of days dealing with Officer Locklin.

The memories were interrupted, though, when Bryce suddenly leaped from the side and swatted at the shot. He deflected it just enough, causing the ball to glance off the side of the rim.

Overtime.

The teams traded baskets for the first two minutes of the three-minute extra period. With 46 seconds on the clock, Bryce committed his fourth foul of the game, sending the Minutemen to the free throw line. The first missed but the second was good, giving Morris a one-point advantage. Having been given an extra timeout because of the overtime, Coach Hammett signaled for it with 34 seconds left.

"Be patient, guys," he said. "When the clock gets to 10 seconds, Ty, take the ball hard to the goal. We'll win it at the free throw line if we need to."

When the clock hit 0:10, Ty faked right and drove to his left. He couldn't possibly get a high percentage shot up and Bryce was covered inside. With five seconds left, Ty spun and kicked the ball out to Will. No Morris player was within 10 feet of him and he let the wide-open three-point attempt fly with three ticks left.

Will immediately saw the shot was short. Way short.

Luckily, Bryce saw the ball falling too quickly. Though pinned by two Minutemen, he managed to stick up his right hand and tap the ball up toward the glass. It bounded softly off the backboard and fell through as the buzzer sounded.

Coach Hammett and the players on the bench sprinted to the floor as the team celebrated the win and the perfect season. Will found Bryce in the pile and pulled him to his feet.

"Greatest play I've ever seen," he shouted over the noise. "We did it!"

Bryce gave Will a quick hug then rejoined the rest of the team.

Will felt a tug on the back of his arm. He turned to see Officer Locklin standing with Steve and Alicia.

"Great game, Will," Officer Locklin said. "Great season!"

"Thanks," Will said. "Bryce saved it for us!"

Officer Locklin nodded proudly, patted Will on the back and went to find his son. Between Steve and Alicia stepped the person Will really wanted to see.

"I'm so proud of you!" Shelby screamed.

Will picked her up, spun her around and hugged her.

"I'm really, really glad you were here," he said.

"So am I, Will Stover! So am I!"

Other books by CE Butler:

Freshman Phenom

Diamond Disaster

Made in the USA
Middletown, DE
25 October 2015